**What if Ellie and Andy got away from words as an effort to heal the breach?**

What if they went back to the beginning of their love affair, where tentative touches and uncertain kisses led gradually into something more…

They'd been too angry and hurt by each other to even consider having sex, the very thought of it not exactly repulsive but something definitely to be avoided—alien, somehow, in the environment between them…

But romance was different.

Would romance work better than words?

Dear Reader,

It has been a while since I did an outback story, but farmers over a large swath of Australia have suffered ten years of drought, while earlier this year most in the far north had the situation worsened by torrential rain that killed tens of thousands of drought-weakened cattle. Outback towns have all suffered, and they struggle to get doctors to work in isolated regions.

So when a couple determined to work in the "bush" as we call it, go out there, they are determined to stay even when tragedy hits them and their marriage falls apart. They work together as well as ever, but the hurt they've caused each other has opened a deep gulf between them. And they both acknowledge, if only to themselves, that they still love the other—that hasn't changed. It's just a matter of bridging the abyss between them. A young visitor forces them closer, and they begin a tentative romance that leads eventually to a love greater than they have ever known, so Christmas is a real time of joy for them and the waifs and strays they have collected on their journey.

I hope you enjoy their journey,

*Meredith Webber*

# THE DOCTORS' CHRISTMAS REUNION

---

MEREDITH WEBBER

ISBN-13: 978-1-335-64193-9

The Doctors' Christmas Reunion

First North American Publication 2019



This edition published by arrangement with Harlequin Books S.A.

For questions and comments about the quality of this book, please contact us at CustomerService@Harlequin.com.

Printed in U.S.A.

**Books by Meredith Webber**

**Harlequin Medical Romance**

***Bondi Bay Heroes***

*Healed by Her Army Doc*

***The Halliday Family***

*A Forever Family for the Army Doc*
*Engaged to the Doctor Sheikh*
*A Miracle for the Baby Doctor*
*From Bachelor to Daddy*

***Wildfire Island Docs***

*The Man She Could Never Forget*
*A Sheikh to Capture Her Heart*

*The Accidental Daddy*
*The Sheikh Doctor's Bride*
*The One Man to Heal Her*
*New Year Wedding for the Crown Prince*
*A Wife for the Surgeon Sheikh*

Visit the Author Profile page
at Harlequin.com for more titles.

**Praise for**
**Meredith Webber**

"The way this story ended had me cheering for this couple's happy ever after…. I would recommend *A Forever Family for the Army Doc* by Meredith Webber if you enjoy the fake relationship trope or a story where the hero and heroine are meant to be."

—*Harlequin Junkie*

# CHAPTER ONE

ELLIE FRASER STUDIED her husband across the breakfast table.

Rather stern profile, with a straight nose and high forehead—until he smiled, of course, when the crinkly lines fanning out from his eyes made you want to smile back at him.

Brown, those eyes were, and she knew them both warm and soft as a cuddly blanket *and* hard as stones.

Dark hair, cut stubble-short—a number one, but due for a cut, so nearly a number two at the moment. It would feel like the fuzz on her old teddy if she ran her hand across it, but it had been a while since that had happened.

And that funny little whorl of hair, just on the hairline above his left eyebrow. A whorl she'd touched so often, twirled around her fingers, back when his hair was longer…

Her heart ached, just from looking at him.

She'd loved Andy. She knew that with the

deep certainty that had been with her from the day he'd asked her to marry him.

She loved him still—she knew that, too—but she had somehow lost him, and along with him the oneness of them as a couple that had seemed so normal for so long.

Ellie and Andy. Andy and Ellie. All through university; through the almost soul-destroying work schedules of their internship; through their volunteer work in Africa—where they'd seen the worst that human beings could do to each other—their oneness had remained. Their goals, dreams and futures had been inextricably entwined in a way she'd thought would never fray, let alone be pulled apart.

And yet right now they couldn't have been further apart, for all that Andy had asked her up to his flat in the top section of the old house to discuss some idea he had about a soccer team that he was setting up, which seemed to be of far more interest to him than the split in their relationship.

Or was it a useful diversion from it?

*She'd* thrown herself into work, but still had far too much time to think of the past and what might have been...

Andy had even cooked her breakfast, though she could have done without the pain that the pretend intimacy of eating together brought with it.

'So I thought I'd have a barbecue here on Saturday—about lunchtime, before the game. Until we get a proper clubroom there's nowhere else. I'll ask some of the older team members to organise the food—just sausages and onions and bread, or bread rolls.' He looked up at her and grinned. 'And, yes, I'll make sure the boys do some of the shopping, not just send the girls.'

*Heaven help me! We've barely spoken for months, apart from work stuff, and still that grin makes my stomach churn...*

Ellie swallowed a sigh along with the last of her toast, left the dirty dishes on the table—after all he *had* invited her as a guest—and made her way downstairs to her own flat, with its well-set-up medical surgery, enclosed under the old timbered home.

Ellie and Andy had moved to Maytown six months ago—she pregnant at last and Andy excited to be back in his home town, doing the job he'd always dreamed of doing: providing medical care for people in the often harsh Outback.

Maytown, a small town in the mid-west, had been established when settlers had brought sheep to the area, although now it was mainly cattle country. A large coal mine, opened twenty kilometres north of the town, had brought in extra business in recent years, with some of the mining families settling in the town while other workers lived in the on-site camp, flying in and flying out from places on the coast, working shifts of two weeks on duty then one week off.

Ellie had become as keen as he was on the town, both from Andy's talk of growing up there and her visits to his family, so they'd leapt on Andy's parents' suggestion they buy the old house and practice. Andy's parents had both been doctors, his mother running the practice, his father working at the hospital. The senior Frasers had wanted to move closer to the coast, cutting back on their workloads as they prepared for retirement.

To Andy and Ellie, it had seemed a magical coincidence—a little bit of serendipity—because they'd both wanted to bring up their longed-for child in the country. And it had been an ideal situation, with Ellie working from the surgery downstairs, knowing when she had the baby she'd get help but would still always be on hand, while Andy took over his father's post at the hospital.

They'd moved in late July, and Ellie had practically danced through the old house, imagining it festooned with Christmas decorations. With the baby due in November, their first Christmas in their new home would be spent celebrating his or her—they hadn't wanted to know the sex—first Christmas, too.

Just the three of them this year, a family…

It should have been perfect.

Until, at twenty-three weeks, when they'd settled in, and everything seemed to be going so well, she'd lost the baby and somehow, in the ensuing pain and anguish, lost Andy, too.

They'd turned to each other for comfort and support in those first hard weeks, and had also discovered that they were part of a very caring community. The local people had helped them through their grief with comforting words and little acts of kindness, flowers left on the front steps, a picture drawn by a kindergarten child, and more food than they could ever eat.

And, slowly, they'd made their way back to a different kind of peace, each wrapped in their private sorrow, but together still.

Until, six weeks after the loss…

Ellie sighed again.

Had she been wrong?

Pushed too hard?

She didn't know.

But when she'd talked to Andy about one last attempt at IVF—not immediately, of course, but when her body was ready—Andy's response had staggered her.

He had been adamant—enraged, really. His answer had been an adamant *no.*

Their two—well, three now—failed IVF attempts had already cost them too much, both financially and emotionally, and no amount of arguing was going to change his mind. He was done.

Completely done.

And if she thought they needed a baby to make their marriage complete then it couldn't be much of a marriage.

Stunned by his pronouncement, Ellie's immediate reaction had been to pack her bags and head back to the city, but she'd grown far too fond of the town and its people to just walk out and leave them without a GP.

Early on, she and Andy had tried to talk—one or other of them calling a truce—but the talk had soon become a row and now too many bitter, hurtful words hung in the air between them. Although Ellie could concede in her head that they would never have a child, she found it so much harder to accept it in her heart.

Even harder to accept that Andy wouldn't consider trying…

So she'd opted to stay, but *had* packed her bags, moving into the flat downstairs, built to house the locums his parents had hired to replace Andy's mother during her own maternity leave.

Did the townspeople know?

Was there gossip?

Ellie assumed they did and that the gossip existed as it did in all country towns, but few attempted to discuss their situation, although she often felt the warmth of their compassion.

The separate living and work situation had turned out for the best, Ellie thought glumly as she made her way through to the surgery and nodded a good morning to Maureen, her receptionist-cum-nurse, who was busy hanging tinsel along the front of her desk.

Dismissing the idea that it could possibly be that close to Christmas when she herself felt so bleak, her thoughts tracked back to Andy... But how were they going to cope with Christmas?

Didn't the very word conjure up togetherness?

Joy and laughter and sharing...

Happiness, and hope for the future...

Could they carry on with Christmas celebrations as if nothing had ever happened? Sit at one of their tables—just the two of them—with silly paper hats on their heads, reading even sillier jokes?

The ache in Ellie's heart deepened, but suddenly she knew.

She couldn't do Christmas, not here, not with Andy—she couldn't go on with things the way they were. If she advertised now, she might find a young doctor, fresh out of GP training, who'd like the challenge of working in the bush. Or a skilled, well-qualified migrant, happy to spend three years working in the country before applying for permanent citizenship.

She was sure there'd be someone.

She wouldn't actually get a new appointee until January, when staff changes were generally made, but if she stayed until just before Christmas, then Andy could manage any emergencies for a week or two.

She'd go—

Where would she go?

Where the hell would she go?

Back to the city?

To what?

Ellie shook her head. That idea had zero appeal to her.

And she'd grown to love this town and its people so maybe she should go to another country town—one without Andy in it!

Ellie could feel her heart weeping at the thought, but she had to accept they couldn't go on as they were.

'What's Andy up to with this soccer club idea of his?'

Maureen interrupted her gloomy thoughts as she pushed the final tack into place on the tinsel and fetched Ellie the mail.

Ellie shook her head, clearing Christmas—and leaving—from her mind.

Why *had* Andy started the soccer club? Had he told her while she was busy checking out all the familiar bits of the man she knew so well? Loved, even?

'I know he's having a barbecue for them on Saturday; our side veranda seems to have become the unofficial clubhouse. And some of the kids I've seen coming and going are far from athletic types, so I guess he's doing it to raise their fitness levels.'

'My Josie's joined,' Maureen said, 'and you know the worry I have with her weight. I would have thought she'd be the last person picked for any team, so maybe fitness is behind it.'

Ellie thought of the motley lot she'd seen on the side veranda from time to time, and for the first time wondered just what Andy *was* up to with this soccer club he'd started. The ones she'd noticed were a very mixed bunch.

There were a couple of gangly Sudanese lads from the group of refugee families who'd been re-settled in the country town, a young teenage girl who was often in trouble with the police, two girls from a remote aboriginal settlement who boarded in town for schooling, and a rather chubby lad she suspected was bullied at school…

Ellie took the mail through to her consulting room, aware yet again of the painful arguments that had split their oneness, and the gulf that had widened between them. Once Andy would have shared his interest in the team, and she'd have shared his enthusiasm…

This was no good, she needed to focus on work.

Ellie scanned the patient list, surprised to see Madeleine Courtney back again. Madeleine was a puzzle—one she would have shared with Andy had things been different.

But they weren't, she reminded herself sharply, stamping down on the little kernel of unhappiness inside her before it could open, overwhelming her with memories and grief…

Only one other name stood out—Chelsea Smith. She frowned, trying to remember a patient of that name, then rubbed at her forehead because she knew she'd be frowning and it wouldn't be long before she had permanent frown lines, and became known as Grumpy Doc Fraser.

'Who's this Chelsea Smith?' she called to Maureen.

'She's a new patient. She phoned earlier so I

put her in that space you leave every morning for emergencies.'

*Thanks a bunch*, Ellie thought, but she didn't say it. New patients always took longer to treat as Ellie had to gather as much information as possible from them.

But Maureen had done the right thing, they made a point of never turning anyone away.

Shrugging off her rambling thoughts, she sorted through the mail, setting bills aside and tossing advertising bumf into the bin.

Andy sat in the tiny space that was his hospital 'office', scanning the internet for videos of soccer coaching, although images of Ellie as she'd sat in the kitchen again kept intruding. The hospital was quiet—too quiet—leaving him far too much time to think of Ellie and the mess their marriage was in.

Shouldn't losing a child have brought them closer together, not thrown up a wall between them?

It was because thinking of Ellie caused him physical pain that he had thrown himself into establishing a Maytown soccer team, allowing soccer to block out all but his most insistent thoughts.

Would their son have played soccer?

The wave of pain that accompanied *that* thought sent Andy back to the videos.

How could he not have known how much it would hurt—losing the baby, losing his son?

He took a deep breath and went back to the videos. He needed to do something constructive and worthwhile.

The call to the emergency room—hardly big enough to deserve the name 'department'—sent him in search of work, which was an even better diversion than the soccer team.

Although the ghost of Ellie always worked beside him, for this had been their dream: to work together in the country, bringing much-needed medical services to people who'd so often had to go without.

The patient was a child, a young boy—maybe twelve—bravely biting his lip to stem the tears while he clutched at his injured side.

'Bloody fence strainers broke,' a man Andy assumed was the father said. 'The barbed wire whipped around him like a serpent. I'm Tim Roberts, and this here's Jonah.'

Andy shook hands with the pair, then leant over to examine the wound. A red weal showed where the wire had hit the boy, but the serious wound was just above his right groin.

'Bit of a barb got in there, but the wife pulled

it out with tweezers and put some cream on it last night, but you can see how it is now.'

The area was red, swollen, and obviously infected.

'I'll need to open it up,' he said. 'We'll just give Jonah light sedation and clean out the wound.'

There was no need to mention there could be damage to the bowel, but Andy would have to look carefully, which was why he'd chosen to give an anaesthetic over a local pain injection.

His mind ran through the roster of staff on duty. Tony was a good theatre nurse but Andrea—who was the only nurse trained to give anaesthetic—was off duty. He'd have to phone Ellie to come in and do it.

And the stupid flip of his heart when he even thought her name reminded him that the love he felt for his wife had never gone away.

Yes, they'd parted—pushed apart by the pain of loss—but the love he felt for her was as strong as ever.

Or was it longing more than love…?

'I won't be able to operate until later,' he told Tim. 'If you've other things to do in town, Jonah will be quite safe here. In fact, he'll probably be thoroughly spoilt by the nurses.

* * *

Ellie was about to tackle her first patient of the day when her cellphone rang.

Her heart leapt when she saw it was Andy.

'Sorry, El, love, but could you grab a half-hour later in the day to do a mild anaesthetic for me? Kid with infection just above the right groin. X-ray shows foreign object in there. He's had breakfast so I'm happy to wait a few hours. How's your day looking?'

Ellie switched back to her patient list.

'I could do eleven-thirty,' she said. 'That would run into my lunch break so there'd be no rush.'

'Grand!'

And he was gone, so suddenly that Ellie found herself peering at her cellphone as if *it*, rather than Andy, had caused the abrupt farewell.

*Grand?*

How could their love have grown so cold that 'grand' had become 'goodbye'?

She was being silly, of course. It had been months since a telephone conversation had finished with 'love you'.

Although he *had* called her 'love', the way he always had done…

*That was just habit*, she told herself firmly and hauled her mind back to work.

For all their separate lives at home, their professional lives had barely changed, their work lives remaining stable as they followed their usual routine, assisting each other when needed, discussing patients they shared.

They were even enjoying the togetherness of that side of things—well, Ellie did and she thought Andy seemed to…

Although that would stop—and soon—if she went ahead and moved.

Even thinking about it caused her pain.

Putting the mail aside for later, she powered up her computer, checked test results that had come in, then switched to her appointments list.

Back in work mode, she speed-read down the appointments, putting asterisks against the patients who'd be coming in for test results so she could be sure she'd re-read the results before the patient arrived.

Busy with the list, she barely heard the outer door open, but Maureen was greeting the first arrival, no doubt handing her the patient information forms to fill in.

She pressed the buzzer, and heard Maureen tell Chelsea to go on through.

It was a pregnant young woman who came in. A *very* young, not *very* pregnant woman, slight and blonde, who seemed strangely familiar.

'Don't I know you?' she asked, smiling at the obviously nervous young woman.

A nod in response.

Ellie smiled again as she asked, 'Do I have to guess how, or will you tell me?'

Another nod, then Chelsea drew in a deep breath.

'I thought Andy might be here,' she said, 'although Aunty Meg always worked here and Uncle Doug at the hospital.'

Aunty Meg, Uncle Doug: Andy's parents?

Light dawned.

'Of course I know you! You're Chelsea Fraser. I'm so sorry I didn't recognise you, but you've kind of grown since you were flower-girl at our wedding. Did you come here to see Andy?'

Chelsea frowned.

'Well, I came to see both of you really. I'm pregnant, you see, and I wondered whether I could stay with you until I have the baby, because you probably heard Mum and Dad split up and Mum's gone off to find herself, whatever that means. She's in India, or maybe Nepal, and Dad's gone to Antarctica again, and Harry—you remember my older brother Harry?—well, he's supposed to be looking after me but he's at uni most of the time or out partying so he's never there.'

'You're all on your own?' Ellie asked.

'Well, Alex—that's my boyfriend—he comes over...'

Tears began to stream down Chelsea's face, and Ellie left her chair to walk around and wrap her arms around the unhappy, lonely child. Ellie held her tightly and let her cry out her tension, handing her the box of tissues when the sobs became hiccups as the tears dried up.

'I didn't mean for this to happen,' Chelsea whispered, patting the bump. 'But I was so lonely and Alex loves me, and I was on the Pill but must have forgotten to take it or something and then I wasn't sure, you see... But of course I *was* pregnant and Alex wanted to tell his parents and have me come and live with them, but then they might think Mum and Dad are really awful parents, and they're not, you know, they've just kind of lost their way.'

*Tell me about it!* Ellie thought, but didn't say, although she did think Chelsea's mother could have waited a little longer to find herself. She shook the thought away and pressed Maureen's buzzer twice to warn her the next appointment would be late.

'They brought us up to be independent,' Chelsea explained, 'and to think for ourselves, but I didn't want everyone at school to know about this, or the cousins and all, so I thought if you and Andy let me stay here until the baby's born, then I can go back to school and no one would know.'

Except there'd be a baby somewhere, Ellie thought, but didn't say.

'No one back home knows because it's been cold and I've been able to wear baggy jumpers back at home. I told my friends my uncle needed me out at his place in the bush and here I am.'

She'd so obviously practised what she was going to say that it came out in a slightly garbled rush, and Ellie had to be careful not to smile.

'Does anyone know where you are?'

Chelsea nodded.

'I told Harry and he thought it was a good idea. He said there wasn't anything Mum or Dad could do to help at the moment and at least I'd be safe with you and Andy.'

'Of course you will be,' Ellie assured her, then, after a niggle of doubt, added, 'I'll have to talk to Andy, but I'm sure he'd be happy to have you. It's not as if there aren't plenty of bedrooms in the old house.'

'And there's the little flat downstairs. We often stayed in it when we came for Christmas.'

*My little flat.*

And with Chelsea here how long would it

take for word to travel along the family grapevine and Andy's parents to realise things had gone wrong between her and Andy? They'd kept it from them while Meg had been going through chemo for breast cancer and they hadn't wanted to heap more worries on her head.

Meg had become more of a friend than a mother-in-law for Ellie, who'd known from the first time she'd met Andy's family that she'd love to be one of their warm, happy household. Her own father was dead, and her mother drifted from one country to another, one man to another, much as Chelsea's mother appeared to be doing. Family had been a big gap in Ellie's life.

So upsetting Meg with the story of their split had never even been a consideration.

And now here was Chelsea, and there was no getting away from it, despite the current circumstances, the Frasers were Ellie's family now, so Chelsea was her responsibility as well as Andy's.

'I should be examining you, not chatting,' she said. 'Do you want to hop up on the couch? Nothing invasive, I just need to feel what's going on then we'll take some blood for tests, and check your blood pressure and pulse, and Maureen will make an appointment for you to come in for a scan later in the week.

'Relax!' she told Chelsea as her patient lay rigid on the couch. 'Do you know how pregnant you might be?'

A quick shake of the head was the only answer.

'No worries!' Ellie told her gently. 'We can do a measure of what we call the fundal height and that will give us an approximate time. It's not entirely accurate, and is a better guide after twenty weeks, but let's see.'

The measurement of fourteen centimetres gave her a gestation period of twelve to sixteen weeks.

'Does that seem about right to you? Can you remember when you had your last period?'

Chelsea shook her head.

'I was so sad and lonely when Mum went away, and then Dad did, too. Alex has been my boyfriend for ages, and he comforted me and stayed over a few times and it just happened.'

*Of course it did*, Ellie thought, but didn't say. Poor kid must have been totally lost, with her parents not only breaking up but taking off. Mum heaven knew where, and Dad—who Ellie remembered now was a climatologist—heading off to the ice and snow at the very bottom of the world.

*I need to talk to Andy.*

This thought had passed through Ellie's head earlier, but now it became insistent.

'Well, you seem totally fit to me,' she told Chelsea, 'and as you know there's plenty of room for you. How did you get here? Did you bring clothes?'

'Train, and not much, to answer both your questions. The train got in this morning, and as far as clothes, I knew it would be hot, and I didn't really know what to get.'

Of course, the train had come in this morning; it was the big weekly event in the town, for it not only brought people but fresh fruit and vegetables.

'Well, how about you go upstairs and choose a room along the back veranda—Andy uses the side one for his soccer club and people come and go along the front one. Have a shower and then, if you're up to it, you could walk uptown—it's only two blocks—and check out the limited array of clothes in the general store. I'll phone them and tell them to put anything you want on our account.'

'Oh, no, I've got my own credit card,' Chelsea protested. 'But I'd like to get a few things.'

'Great! And when you get back you can help yourself to anything in the kitchen. There's bread and ham and cheese for sandwiches, and plenty of salad things. I might be late back for lunch as I have to help Andy with an op, but just look after yourself. And come and see Maureen down here if you need to ask anything. I know that doesn't sound very hospitable, but I've got patients all morning. Will you be okay?'

To Ellie's surprise, Chelsea flung her arms around her neck and hugged her hard, tears in her voice as she said, 'You've been so kind. I know I don't deserve it, but I'm really grateful!'

'Of course you deserve it,' Ellie said, a little choked up herself. 'You're family!'

How best to help her?

What would Andy advise?

# CHAPTER TWO

SHE SET ALL thoughts of Chelsea—*and* Andy—aside as she went through her list of morning patients, pleased with some, concerned about others, mostly elderly men who seemed more aimless and depressed than ill. In other places, they could have a community garden or an allotment to work on, but out here, where water was a very scarce commodity, such a thing would be a luxury.

But her thoughts returned to Chelsea as she walked briskly to the hospital, sighing as she went in through the side entrance, where more Christmas decorations were already in place.

But Christmas cheer was the last thing on her mind as she considered the discussion she'd have to have with Andy.

Not right now, when there'd be other people around, but later on they would definitely need to talk.

Chelsea's arrival had thrown their arrangement into disarray. It had seemed sensible to live separately within the house, mainly to avoid gossip and speculation, but Chelsea would pick up on it immediately, and word would spread around the family, and Ellie knew it would cause distress to Meg.

She pushed into the theatre changing room and found Andy already waiting for her.

'Sorry, I was held up on my first patient and I've been late all morning,' she explained.

His beautiful Ellie looked so tired and stressed that Andy wanted nothing more than to take her in his arms and hold her—to find their way back to where they'd been. But pain and grief and too many harsh words had opened up a gulf between them, and as yet, he could find no way of bridging it.

And did he even want to?

He shook his head. That was a stupid question when there was a patient waiting.

Of course he wanted to! The thought of living without Ellie was…well, inconceivable.

'The patient is a young lad who got hit by a strand of barbed wire when he was helping his father repair a fence. Apparently, the fence strainers snapped, the wire flicked back, and a piece flew into his lower abdomen. They got it out, and cleaned and dressed the wound, but there's a bit still in there—one of the barbs, I'd say—and it's badly infected. I need to go in and clean it out before it develops into sepsis. He's on IV antibiotics, and I'll leave a drain in place for a few days if it looks at all dubious.'

Andy watched as Ellie greeted Tony, a nurse who loved theatre work, then checked the drugs and instruments he'd laid out for her.

Once upon a time, in what seemed like another life—in another country, for that matter—they'd worked together like this. The lack of specialist doctors in some of the African countries where they'd lived meant you had to do whatever was required of you, and often it was surgery—he cutting while Ellie did the anaesthetic—basic though it had been.

He held back a snort, disgusted that he could be distracted by such trivial thoughts. All that was so far in the past it was history now.

Yet how could he not watch as she spoke quietly to the boy, explaining how he'd be getting sleepy, checking the cannula already attached to the back of one small hand and smiling gently. She was so good with children—the children they would never have…

Satisfied that all was well, Ellie took up the prepared anaesthetic, and with a nod to Andy injected it, waiting until the boy dozed off before securing the oxygen mask over his mouth and nose.

How many times—?

*Enough!*

The past belonged in the past. Here and now, he needed one hundred percent concentration on Jonah. Electrodes already attached to his patient's body told the monitor everything was stable, and Ellie would keep an eye on it while he cut carefully into the pale skin on the lower abdomen, Tony beside him to mop the blood and cauterise any small bleeders.

Andy glanced across the table, and by chance met Ellie's eyes above her mask. She winked at him—something she'd done a thousand times before—a 'going well' kind of wink, but the sight of such a silly, insignificant facial tic brought an arrow of pain into his innermost being. One he tried to ignore…

The infection was obvious, the culprit a small piece of metal—a tiny scrap had broken free from a barb on the wire. No wonder the boy had been complaining of pain.

Andy irrigated the wound and searched for any secondary sites of infection, but everything was clean and clear.

'I won't leave a drain,' he said, as much to himself as to the staff around the table. 'In that position it could be easily dislodged, especially considering he's an adventurous young boy.'

He closed the wound, and nodded to Ellie to reverse the anaesthetic, then stood back while Tony did the dressing.

He should go and change. This team knew what they were doing. The boy would be transferred to a bed and wheeled through to the small recovery room. Ellie was in charge of him now and would be watching over him until he was fully conscious and aware of his surroundings.

But sometimes Andy needed to watch his wife—to watch and wonder what had happened to them to end up on either side of what was now an abyss.

Was it his fault?

Those final, hurtful words about the state of their marriage had certainly marked the end of life as they'd known it, but what had brought them to that?

Did he still feel a lingering resentment about the money the IVF had cost?

But it had been he who'd first suggested IVF, so it couldn't be that that burned inside him.

Yet *something* did.

He'd been keen to have a family—as keen as Ellie was—but that had been back before he'd known about the pain of loss; how much each failure would hurt, although that was nothing compared to the terrible piercing pain of losing the baby.

But worst of all had been watching Ellie's pain and being unable to take it away from her. *That* was the part he'd found so bloody impossible…

It wasn't that she'd pushed him away at the time, more that she'd wrapped herself inside it—made a cocoon of her pain—and had no longer been part of him, no, of *them*, cutting their oneness…

Now Andy watched Ellie sadly as she followed the trolley out of the theatre, before heading for the shower. There was nothing like water to wash away pointless suppositions and what-ifs that were too late…

Ellie waited as the youngster came around, checked he was sufficiently conscious to be given a few sips of water, and tell her who and where he was, then she departed, hurrying now, as she'd been due to see a patient at one-thirty and it was already close to two.

But her thoughts remained firmly stuck on Andy.

His skill as a surgeon was undeniable, and while still at university he'd even considered making a career of it, but during their time in Africa he'd realised that his skill lay with people; with helping them, comforting them and, yes, healing them when it was humanly possible.

And it had fired his determination to return to the isolated regions of Australia—areas always crying out for doctors—where his patients would be people he would get to know and care about, not simply a person needing an appendectomy or a new knee.

Ellie caught up as she worked through the afternoon's patients, so had seen the last one out when Chelsea returned, laden with bags and filled with excitement.

'You should rest,' she told the young woman as she locked the surgery door then walked up the front steps and along the veranda to the room Chelsea had chosen.

It had belonged to one of Andy's sisters, and although Ellie had put fresh sheets on the bed in case of unexpected visitors, she'd done little in the way of redecorating, so it still had posters of old rock bands on the walls and a bookcase full of science-fiction books that the whole Fraser family had loved to read.

Ellie half-smiled, remembering how she'd felt an utter alien herself among people who knew a genre she'd never read as well as the Frasers knew sci-fi.

After depositing Chelsea's few possessions,

Ellie showed her the nearest bathroom, then led her into the kitchen.

'You'll probably remember that the kitchen is the centre of the house, it's where we mainly live,' she said, adding rather ruefully, 'That's when we're actually at home.'

And living together... She *had* to talk to Andy!

She'd barely finished the thought when her cellphone buzzed in her pocket.

'Can you come back up, Ellie? Jonah's temperature has shot up, and his heart rate is ninety-five. I'm afraid I must have missed something and he could be heading into sepsis.'

'I'll be right there.'

She looked at Chelsea, new in town, still uncertain of her welcome, and crossed the room to give her a hug.

'I hate having to leave you like this on your first day here but I have to go up to the hospital, and from what Andy said I could be a while,' she said. 'There's food in the fridge, or you could walk up the road and get a burger and chips. The TV in the sitting room only has a couple of channels, but feel free to use it, and there are plenty of books around the place. Do you think you'll be okay?'

'Don't worry about me,' Chelsea assured her. 'I sat up all night on the train and I'm exhausted. If it's all right with you, I'll just get a drink of milk and a sandwich and go straight to bed.'

'Bless you,' Ellie said. 'But I'll leave both my and Andy's numbers and if you're at all worried about anything, please phone one of us.'

'I'll be fine,' Chelsea assured her. 'I *have* stayed here before and I know my aunt and uncle were often called out at night. You go and do your work.'

But as Ellie walked swiftly up the road to the hospital, she couldn't help thinking of the young woman alone in the big house, and wonder just what she was thinking, not to mention what Andy was going to make of it all…

She arrived to find Andrea, a senior nurse who had specialist anaesthetic training, already in Theatre.

'I'll need you to assist,' Andy said, as Ellie walked in. 'There's gear set out in the anteroom, and Tony will help you scrub.'

Ellie took a deep breath. It wasn't that she hadn't assisted in operations before. It was part of their medical training, and they'd done a lot in Africa, but surgery had always made her feel anxious, as if she had no business having her hands in someone else's body. It was impersonal, yet at the same time deeply moving.

Shaking away the thoughts, she changed, scrubbed her hands and arms and held them up for Tony to slide on the gloves. He tied an extra apron around her waist, and she was ready.

'Will you enlarge the wound you made earlier?' she asked Andy as she took her place beside him.

A quick headshake.

'It was big enough, but I must have missed something.'

The tightness of his voice told her how stressed he was—stressed because he felt he'd somehow failed the boy.

'There was nothing obvious,' she reminded him, 'and you didn't want to interfere with his bowel by poking around under it.'

She paused then added, in a deep, terrifying voice, 'Never touch the bowel.'

Andy laughed. Her mimicry of a lecturer they'd had in third year had always been good, and the words took him back to when, as students, they and their friends had used the words in more earthy ways.

It broke his tension and he opened the wound, holding it for her to clamp so he had a clear view.

'Think about the barb,' he muttered, and although she knew he was talking to himself, she understood what he was getting at. The barb could have pierced a muscle, tendon or even the bowel, and infection had developed in the second site.

But there was nothing obvious. Lecturer or not, he was going to have to touch the bowel.

He gently lifted the nearest coil of the large intestine, checking all around it for damage.

Nothing.

They irrigated the wound again, and closed it up, then all stood frowning at the monitor, which had no good news for them.

'Hang on,' Ellie said. 'Didn't someone say he was fixing a barbed-wire fence? Imagine what happened. The fence strainers broke, the loose wire would have flicked back, one barb would have pierced his skin. How far apart are the barbs on barbed wire?

'Roughly a hand span.' It was Andy who answered, catching on quickly to Ellie's train of thought.

So some things hadn't changed…

'That means the next barb would be here,' he said, measuring across the boy's abdomen with his hand.

They all peered at the spot but there was no sign of damage to the skin, or any indication of infection.

'Imagine him with clothes on,' Ellie said. 'Jeans, most likely, and low slung how the kids wear them these days. That barb would have hit the double layer of the pocket, possibly even a stud, so the next barb would be here...' She used her hand to measure the distance, brushing Andy's hand then glancing up, meeting his eyes above his mask—a flash of something as sudden and powerful as lightning flashing between them. 'If the wire wrapped around him.'

They found the wound beneath their patient's left hip, a tiny pinprick of a mark, surrounded by swollen, angry redness.

While Tony went for the portable X-ray machine, Ellie and Andy propped the boy on his side, careful not to touch each other after whatever it was that had flashed between them earlier.

'From the size of it, it's just an infection rather than another foreign object,' Ellie said, and Andy nodded, although she could tell he was furious with himself for not checking more carefully earlier.

She opened her mouth to say, 'You weren't to know,' but Andrea beat her to it.

Not that Andy would have found any comfort in the assurance. He prided himself on his physical examination of all patients, although earlier this morning the pinprick of a mark could have been all but invisible.

The X-ray showed no foreign matter in the

wound, but Andy opened it up anyway. Clearing out the infection already there would lead to a quicker recovery for the boy.

'Do you still hate it?' Andy asked Ellie as they left the hospital an hour later. It was only when she didn't reply that he looked around to find she'd halted, twenty or so paces behind him, and was gazing up at the night sky.

'Still gets to you, huh?' he teased as he walked back to join her, resting his hand on the small of her back as he had so often in the past. Often just a touch in passing, often a prelude—but he wouldn't go there.

She smiled at him.

'I just cannot believe how many stars there are. I know they are there, in the city and we just don't see them for the other lights, but out here…'

She waved her arms around as if to encompass the beauty she couldn't put into words.

'And all yours,' Andy said, wondering if she remembered his promise to give her the moon and the stars…

And looking at her, her clear skin luminous in the starlight, her golden-brown hair framing a face he'd always thought perfection, he wanted to take her in his arms again, take her back to that time, make her really his once more.

'Did you ask me something?'

Her question broke the moment, although he knew the moment he'd felt had never been possible.

Thought back to his question.

'Oh, I just wondered if you still hated surgery?'

She'd started forward but now paused again, turned back to him.

'I've never really *hated* it so much as felt very uncomfortable. It seems so intrusive to be fumbling around inside someone else's body.'

Ellie sighed, and shook her head as if to chase the thoughts away.

'And speaking of bodies, I really need to talk to you about something that came up today. Shall we get a pizza and sit in the park to eat it?'

'You've hidden a dead body somewhere, and need my help to bury it?' Andy said, hoping the teasing words hid a sudden panic inside him.

Was she tired of their pretend marriage?

Was she leaving him completely?

Did she want a divorce?

*Nonsense!* he told himself. She'd mentioned bodies. It was something from work she wanted to discuss.

But the tension she'd aroused remained with him as he ordered their pizza, half with anchovies and half without, took extra paper napkins as they'd be eating in the park, and waited while Ellie chatted with the young girl behind the counter, blithely unaware of the torment her words had caused him.

Their marriage as a marriage might be virtually over, but could he live without the woman he loved?

The woman, he was fairly certain, who still loved him?

And could their marriage really be over?

He thought of the times when they'd tried to talk about it, as two intelligent people working out their differences. But the problem with loving someone was that you knew their sore and vulnerable spots—knew the words that would stab them in those places…

Worse still, you used those words as weapons.

So not talking had seemed easier, although Ellie deciding to make the move downstairs had left him feeling hollowed out inside. He was aware it could be a prelude to her leaving altogether for all she'd said they both needed their own space for a while.

Andy carried the pizza up to the park, which was deserted at this time of night, and set it down on a table, aware as he always was of Ellie's warmth by his side.

But worry about this 'talk' now nibbled at his

mind so, as he placed a piece of pizza—from the anchovies' side—on a napkin, and passed it to his wife, he said, 'Okay, talk. What's up?'

Ellie turned, questions in her night-dark eyes, and he realised he'd spoken too abruptly.

'Right!' she began, apparently reading his anxiety in his face. 'Chelsea arrived this morning—your cousin Chelsea—and she's pregnant and wanted to get away from home and people who know her until after the baby's born. Apparently both her parents are off somewhere and Harry's been looking after her—'

'Not very well, if she's pregnant!' Andy muttered. 'Does he know she's here?'

'Apparently so,' Ellie said, 'although I will phone him when we get home to tell him she's arrived safely. I tried earlier but his phone was switched off.'

'But where's her mother, for heaven's sake? I know her father's probably off saving whales somewhere, but her mum? And Harry's what? All of nineteen, I imagine, and far more involved in his own life at university than caring for his sister. Of all the irresponsible—'

He realised he was yelling now and it really wasn't Ellie he should be yelling at, but she simply smiled at him and said, 'She's off finding herself, apparently.'

'Mad, they're both mad, they always have

been. How Dad and Ken can possibly be brothers beats me. And as for Jill, why isn't she at home, looking after a kid who's barely out of childhood? I would have thought teenage years were when young girls, in particular, needed their mothers around.'

'She's sixteen,' Ellie told him, 'and twelve to sixteen weeks gestation. A bit hard to be precise at that stage and she has a very slight build.'

She paused, and Andy wondered what worried her about the situation. Apart from it being Chelsea. Teenage pregnancy was far from uncommon these days.

Was she thinking of their arrival here in town—of the coincidence of her being sixteen weeks pregnant when they'd first begun their move to Maytown?

Andy watched as Ellie ate her slice of pizza, chewing and swallowing it before she smiled at him, then shrugged as if uncertain where to begin.

'I can understand her turning to a boyfriend for comfort, with her parents gone, and that the pregnancy was an accident, but I didn't want to push her to talk too much about the future.'

He saw the worry in the little crease between her eyebrows, and read it in her voice.

'The thing is, Andy, we'll take her in, I was

sure you'd agree with that, but I wondered if she—if we…'

It was so unlike Ellie to be this hesitant over something that he reached out and took her hand, feeling her fingers curl into his, warm and sticky from the pizza but accepting his support.

'I wouldn't like your mum to find out about our marriage right now and be upset, which she will if I'm downstairs and you're upstairs while Chelsea's with us. I mean, it's a bit like shouting it to the world.'

Her head lifted so she could watch his face as he considered it.

'Easily fixed,' Andy said, barely suppressing his delight because the top part of the house was desperately empty without Ellie in it. A cool, contained and even frosty Ellie was better than no Ellie at all.

If only he'd realised that before she'd made the move downstairs. He should have talked to her about feeling shut out; about his own pain, and how much it had frightened him; about feeling cast adrift after she left —

'You'll move back up? I'm still sleeping in Dad's old room, so you can go back into Mum's.'

She half smiled and he guessed that life in the downstairs flat hadn't been entirely joyous either.

'I didn't take all that much,' she said, 'but, yes, I think that would be best.'

'And Chelsea? Has she planned anything beyond escaping to Maytown for the period of her pregnancy?'

Ellie shrugged.

'We barely talked, and right now she's confused, and lost, and really needs to know she's safe and loved and cared for. I do wonder about Jill going off like that when Chelsca is still so young. Do you think because her husband is always off somewhere, she felt it was her turn?'

Andy grinned at her.

'Who knows what goes on in other people's relationships?' he said, and she responded with a small smile, turning her fingers so she could squeeze *his* hand.

'Too true. Look at ours!' she said with a smile.

The smile and something in her tone of voice suggested there was more hope than defeat in the words but before he could pursue it, Ellie was talking again.

'Well, all we can do is be there for her. I can only help her with her pregnancy at the moment, and perhaps you and I can both talk with her about the future. About the baby, maybe—'

'No!'

The word seemed to echo around the park,

far too loud, far too strong, far too emotionally charged…

Andy breathed deeply, counted to ten then another five, and regained a semblance of control over the dark fear that had seized him.

'I know she's family and I'm happy to take her in, but just what is going to happen to the baby when it arrives? Will you want to keep it, too? Is this your way of getting back at me for refusing more IVF? How long before you start thinking of it as your baby?'

Obviously, the counting hadn't helped because he was shouting now. Ellie's face looked white and strained in the gloom.

The silence that fell between them was somehow louder than his words, broken only when Ellie stood up and said quietly, 'I was only thinking we might help her. Yes, take her in, she's family. It's up to her to decide about the baby but while she's with us we might both be able to help her find a path ahead—at least begin to plan for her future.'

She stepped backwards away from the bench she'd been sitting on, and turned away, pausing only to say, 'And it was *our* baby I wanted, Andy, not someone else's.'

# CHAPTER THREE

HOW HAD THEY gone from hand-holding to being back at war? From what had felt almost like old times to cold apartness?

Andy caught up with her as she stormed away, his long strides easily covering the ground he'd lost.

But getting past his careless words wouldn't be as easy. There'd been no mistaking the raw pain in her voice, even months after they'd lost their baby.

'I'm sorry,' he began, wondering why the words sounded less meaningful than they would have if his arms had been around her, holding her as he whispered them into her ear.

But he did touch her shoulder, draw her closer, so he could look into her eyes.

'Of course we'll help Chelsea decide what she wants to do.' He ploughed on, realising this wasn't such a great idea as Ellie's lips were right there in front of him, and so damn kissable.

He needed to take a deep breath and walk on. He needed to walk and talk, not stop and kiss…

'I imagine she'll be at school during the day, and hopefully she can make some friends before the end of term.'

But Ellie, he realised, was no longer by his side. This time she'd stopped several paces back and was muttering to herself.

'You okay?' he asked.

'Yes!' Ellie caught up with him. 'I just hadn't thought about school. Chelsea's only sixteen so of course she should still be at school.'

She hesitated again.

'Although maybe sixteen is an acceptable age to leave school—I'll have to find out. And will going to school, being pregnant in a place full of strangers, be frightening for her?'

Andy imagined a pregnant Chelsea having to brave it up in front of a room full of teenage strangers. Guilt at his earlier reaction ate into him. Wasn't their profession meant to be a caring one?

Then he smiled as the answer came to him.

'Well, if she's with us for the weekend, she can join in the soccer barbecue. Most of the team are at the high school. They're all good kids, they'll look after her.'

'Oh, Andy! That's a wonderful idea,' the

woman he loved replied, with such enthusiasm that she threw her arms around him and gave him a hug.

It was just a quick hug, and maybe it was the shock of it that stopped him returning it, or the thought of it turning it into something longer, more intimate. There was that kiss idea again…

The mere thought of kissing Ellie made his head spin.

But it was not to be. Although it did seem to Andy that maybe they could make their way back to being friends—something that had seemed impossible when the emotion-driven arguments had sent her off to sleep downstairs two long months ago.

Back then, he hadn't realised just how broken things had become between them, possibly because his mother had often sought refuge from her loud and boisterous family by escaping to the downstairs flat. Even when they had both been upstairs, his parents, in his memory, had never shared a bedroom, his mother being a light sleeper and his father often being called out in the middle of the night.

After a while he'd accepted it was easier this way—easier to have Ellie in a separate space even if he lay awake at night wondering if she, too, was awake.

Wondering if she, too, was thinking of their first night together, of their wedding night…

Sharing a bed and not sharing love, *that* would have been impossible…

'You're really okay about having Chelsea to stay?' Ellie asked, linking her arm through Andy's as they walked through their gate, down the path, and stopped at the bottom of the steps that led up to the veranda.

'Of course I am. Though we should do something about one of the girls' rooms to make it comfortable for her.'

'Or let her do it up how she wants it. It will give her something to do over the holidays and I think she'd probably enjoy it.'

'You're a good woman, Ellie Fraser,' Andy said, his voice curling into her ears, the deep tone finding its way into her heart.

'You're not so bad yourself, for a bloke!' she parried, afraid, because what was happening inside her felt a little bit like falling in love, or the tentative, fragile, beginning part of falling in love, *again*.

She'd worked out, back when their world had crashed, that it was okay to still love Andy—that would never change—but it would be better not to be 'in love' with him, because that would make the gulf between them too hard to bear.

'You might want to check on Chelsea, while I move my things back into your mother's room,' Ellie said. 'She was going to grab something to eat and go to bed, but if she's awake I know she'd like to see you and know you're happy to have her here.'

And being downstairs, packing what few things she'd actually moved, would give Ellie time to think about her feelings for Andy, something that was easier to do when he wasn't around, his body sending messages to hers, reminding her of what they'd had.

She had to think, too, about the decision she'd made so recently—the one to give up and go back to the city.

She could hardly do that with Chelsea here, and become yet another person leaving her in the lurch!

She watched Andy take the steps two at a time and turn along the veranda, peering into rooms to find their guest.

She'd shower downstairs then gather up her things. Upstairs, they'd share the en suite bathroom, as they had when he'd shifted into his father's room.

Back then, in the beginning of the separation, any physical contact between them had actually seemed uncomfortable—dangerous even—but these days, close proximity, particularly in a hug of all things, was reminding her body of the passion they'd shared, and sending little flares of desire skittering along her nerves.

Had he felt it, too?

He certainly hadn't hugged her back, or swung her around the way he used to…

He'd smelled like Andy when she'd hugged him, the faintest lingering scent of his aftershave reminding her—

The thoughts followed her to bed, where she lay wondering about love and loving and sex and Chelsea until, in the middle of a totally unconnected thought about her mother's recipe for Christmas pudding, she fell asleep.

Having found his young cousin fast asleep in one of his sister's rooms, Andy headed for the kitchen and made a cup of tea. He momentarily considered calling to Ellie to see if she wanted one, then remembered the way his body had reacted when she'd hugged him.

It was far better to concentrate on soccer, and focus his mind on doing his best for the makeshift team he was building…

He closed his eyes and cleared his mind, then sat down at the kitchen table with a large notebook in which he was devising soccer practice strategies for his team. With the help of numerous internet videos, he felt he was getting closer to being able to call himself a coach.

At least Andy had help from Madeleine Courtney, one of the high-school teachers, who claimed to have learned soccer coaching. But as her system seemed to consist of dividing the participants into two teams and letting them go at it, he had his doubts about its effectiveness.

His soccer club had started as something he could get his teeth into to stop himself thinking about Ellie and the mess their life was in.

For the first few weeks he hadn't bothered too much about skills or techniques, concentrating on getting the participants interested enough to keep coming. Which had simply meant playing.

But now he wanted more of them than that. There was an inter-town competition beginning in the New Year, with a trial game this weekend, and he wanted them competitive, keen to win, but able to lose gracefully.

Some of these kids had had very little discipline at home, and too much time on their hands. The local police sergeant had introduced him to five of them, so in reality they were doing time for misdemeanours. If he, Andy, could get them fit and interested in the game, who knew where it could lead?

Three others, two girls and a boy, had been brought to Outpatients by their parents because his father had started a weight-loss group and he, Andy, had been prepared to continue it.

But in his opinion, playing sport would not only help their weight loss and build healthy muscle, it would improve their self-esteem as well.

It was win-win, all the way…

But it was up to Andy to get it right. And for that he needed practice strategies for dribbling and passing, things he could easily demonstrate to the kids so they could practise them in their correct positions. And, of course, he needed to teach them the rules. It was one of the reasons he'd arranged the barbecue—so they could have a sit-down session on the veranda going over the rules, and the importance of them in the game, before they ate.

*And* played.

Should pregnant women—girls—play soccer? Another player would even up his numbers. Even if Chelsea only stood in goal, she'd be handy.

He'd have to check.

Or maybe he could ask Ellie…

He was an idiot. He was only plunging himself into this challenge so he didn't have to think about Ellie.

Or the mess he'd made of things between them…

It would be impossible to have her on the team.

He should think about soccer, not Ellie.

It had become a kind of mantra to keep him sane.

Andy divided up his players into two teams and marked out their positions—four defenders, four midfielders and two forwards, plus a goalie for each team, or for one team if he couldn't persuade their new housemate to play.

He wrote out a programme for warming up, some aerobic exercise, and then the drills he wanted them to do. If they worked this way two days a week, they could then have a game after warm-up on Friday. This would be a practice game—a rehearsal for Saturday afternoon—when more and more parents and other spectators were turning up to watch the newly minted Maytown Soccer Team.

In fact, they could do some of the drills on the old tennis court area here at home, which would mean they'd be less likely to skive off into an impromptu game.

And he'd appoint Rangi, one of the Sudanese lads, as his offsider to run the programmes on afternoons he couldn't make it or was running late.

Satisfied that he had, at last, brought a little structure to the group, Andy put away his notebook and headed for bed, wondering if Ellie might get interested in the team even if she wasn't playing. Pictured them together on the sidelines, as one again…

He sighed as he went to bed—alone—and shut his mind against all the questions that were too dangerous to consider: all the *what if I'd done this or said that*, all the useless, totally impossible, ever-haunting *what-ifs*…

Although knowing Ellie was back in the bed they'd shared helped chase the dark thoughts away.

He had nearly kissed her, and he could practically hear her breathing…

Ellie woke early, showered, and dressed for work, then went to check on their new lodger.

Chelsea was up and dressed, sitting on the bed as if uncertain what to do next.

'Come on,' Ellie said to her. 'You'll have to learn to treat this house as your home, and to a certain extent look after yourself because Andy and I are often called out and you'll starve if you can't manage.'

She opened the pantry and pointed to a range of cereal, tea-bags, coffee, even drinking chocolate.

'And there are always eggs and bacon in the fridge if you like a cooked breakfast, but it will be a case of help yourself because we tend to get up, eat, then go to work.'

Chelsea settled on cereal, while Ellie made toast for herself and a pot of tea that she set on the table, along with mugs, milk, and sugar.

'Will you be okay here on your own while we're at work?' she asked, and Chelsea smiled at her.

'I'm just so happy to have a home. Ours was so lonely without Mum and Dad. Harry was hardly ever there. I'll sort out my things then sit on the veranda and read a book. From what I've seen, the Fraser passion for sci-fi is alive and well in this house.'

Ellie shuddered.

'It was totally foreign to me when I first met Andy, and I've never got caught up in it, although I have read some of it.'

At lunchtime, when she and her new boarder sat together in the kitchen, Chelsea explained she was old enough to leave school but she really hadn't wanted to. She'd always wanted to be a scientist so she desperately wanted to finish her schooling, and if possible get into a university.

'How much school have you missed now?' Ellie asked her.

The girl frowned as she worked out her answer.

'About three—maybe five—weeks,' she said. 'I just sat around wishing it would all go away.'

'And if you went back to school here, could you make that up?'

'You mean now, this year, before the end of term—with this?'

She patted her bump.

'Why not?' Ellie said. 'Even if you go back long enough to get some work to do over the Christmas holidays that will catch you up, then you can go back full time next year.'

'And when the baby comes?'

Ellie sighed.

'That's going to depend on what you want to do about the baby. You don't have to make any decisions right now, but there are really only two choices.'

'Keeping it or adoption?'

Tears filled the girl's eyes.

'We've plenty of time to sort that out,' Ellie told her. 'We'll talk about it, you and me, and Andy. Your boyfriend, Alex, too. Talk to him. He should have some say. Between the lot of us we'll work out what's best for both of you.'

Ellie pushed back her chair as she stood up, needing to get back to work and not yet ready for tearful discussions about the baby's future.

Any baby's future…

'If you wouldn't mind clearing away our

plates, then you could have a good look at your room, maybe take down the old posters. You'd better roll them up and put them away somewhere in case they turn out to be precious to their former owner. We can get some paint to freshen up the walls and some new bed linen for you.'

The tears Ellie had been hoping to avoid arrived in full flood, along with mutterings of 'too good to me,' and 'you're too kind'.

But Ellie was already heading down the steps.

'Have a shower and a lie down. You'll feel a lot better after you've had a rest.'

The afternoon was blessedly free of any drama, and she even had one cancellation, which gave her a few minutes to think about her concern for the elderly men in town. Her grandmother had regularly attended a sewing, knitting, and craft group once a week in the hall at a local church, going along for a chat more than the knitting or sewing. The Country Women's Association—an institution in Australia—provided for the women as well, but finding something for the men might prove more difficult.

Many of the local farmers retired to houses in the town, leaving their sons to run the property, and things like indoor bowls or card games might be too tame for them.

A Men's Shed, that was what she needed, but one with a purpose. She'd talk to Andy about it tonight.

And the ease with which that thought came out startled her enough to spend the rest of the afternoon with her mind focussed fully on work.

Which was just as well, as her next patient presented with a racing pulse and a pallor that would make cream look suntanned. Bill Stevens had a history of atrial fibrillation which was usually controlled by his medication. He'd sensibly bought an app for his phone that could tell him when he was in AF, so he could take three more tablets, upping his medication from one hundred to a total of four hundred mgs.

'It usually works for me,' he told Ellie plaintively.

'Well, maybe it still will,' she told him, 'but I'd prefer it if you were in hospital. If it doesn't settle down, they can give you the drug intravenously, and keep you on a monitor so they know what's happening. How did you get here?'

'My wife drove me. She's doing some shopping while she's in town.'

The 'while she's in town' reminded Ellie that many of her patients came from properties up to eighty miles away, and although she knew Bill was closer than that, she certainly didn't want him out there with his heart still playing up, risking a stroke unless they stabilised it. She pressed the buzzer that would bring Maureen into the room.

'Would you please phone an ambulance for Bill, then keep an eye out for his wife. She'll be back when she finishes shopping and we need to let her know he's gone to hospital.'

'Will I phone and let them know he's coming?' Maureen asked.

'No, I'll do it. Andy can access Bill's file there but I'd like to fill him in on today's situation.'

'And if we don't get it back in rhythm with medication?' Andy asked, when Ellie had explained that Bill was on his way.

'Are you up for a cardioversion or will you fly him out?'

Andy peered at the phone for a moment. Was Ellie really asking him that?

Okay so he'd trained in the use of the defibrillator—hadn't they all? He'd even used one to re-start a patient's heart. But the difference with cardioversion was that it had to be synchronised to a particular point in the heart's rhythm, and although the machine itself did that job quite efficiently, as long as you pressed the sync button before shocking, he felt uneasy about it.

If something were to go wrong—if Bill had a seizure when they shocked him—what back-up did he have? One anaesthetic-trained nurse and Ellie at a pinch. No cardiologist for hundreds of miles.

'Send him to the coast,' he heard Ellie's voice say, coming from afar as he still had the phone in his hand in front of him, not up to his ear. 'Presumably he's had lunch, which means you can't anaesthetise him for a few hours, so far better to have a specialist do it. He should be at your hospital by now, I'll send his wife on there. She can either fly out with him or drive to wherever they're taking him. Maybe do neither. If all goes well, they'll send him back tomorrow or the next day, whenever they have an ambulance car coming this way.'

Andy was grinning as he hung up. Ellie was so far ahead of him in some ways, you'd think it was she who'd grown up in the bush with its limited facilities, not him. But everything she said made sense. The state-funded ambulance system had several helicopters used for ferrying patients from outlying districts to specialist hospitals.

He went to meet Bill and explain what was going to happen, asking Andrea, who was on duty in the small ED, to phone for the air ambulance.

'It'll fix itself, it always does,' Bill argued as Andy removed the ambulance leads, replacing them with hospital ones and attaching them to the monitor. Bill's heart rate was still spiking around the one hundred to one hundred and twenty mark, the line occasionally dropping down to ninety-five at the lowest.

'When did you take the extra dose?' he asked Bill, who looked mutinous for a moment, then finally admitted it had been first thing in the morning. That he'd woken with his heart bouncing around in his chest.

'Well, that's what it always feels like,' he added, and Andy nodded, imagining how frightening it must feel even to people who'd experienced it before.

He saw Bill safely away, returning home much later to find Chelsea in the kitchen.

Oh, Andy,' she said, spinning around with a half-peeled potato in her hand and enveloping him in a tight hug. 'Thank you so much for having me. Ellie's been so kind, and I'll try not to be a nuisance, see…'

She held out the potato.

'I'm fixing the veggies for dinner!'

He eased out of her embrace and smiled at her.

'You don't have to earn your keep here,' he said gently. 'After all, we're family.'

Laughter greeted his pronouncement.

'I know but I love cooking, so if you and Ellie don't mind, I might do some now and then.'

'I'm sure neither of us will mind, we're often so tired it's a choice between Thai or Chinese takeaway.'

'It's bad for your health, too much takeaway,' his young cousin said sternly.

Andy laughed.

'You're right, but apart from cooking to keep us healthy, I'm hoping you might be a help to me in another way. Do you know anything about soccer?'

'I was in a team back home, and I played at school,' she said. 'Do you think it would hurt the baby if I played?'

'I'll check that out. I imagine the baby wouldn't be too happy being hit with a soccer ball. But you could be goalie. None of them are good enough to score many goals yet, but you could yell advice to them if they got close. And if a ball actually comes near you, you could always hide behind the post.'

'Not that I'll fit behind a post for much longer,' Chelsea said, and returned to peeling potatoes.

He watched her for a moment, then said, 'When you've finished those, would you mind sitting down with me to look at the drills I've been working out? I only know the game from school, where it didn't seem to matter what you did, but I've watched about a thousand internet videos on coaching it.'

She put down the peeled potato and came towards him, wiping her hands on an old apron of Ellie's she'd put on.

'Let's see what you've got.'

She stood over his shoulder and read what he'd set out, with stick-figure illustrations, and smiled.

'For someone who only played the game at school, that's excellent. You could probably give your forwards more goal-kicking practice. Your two forwards should be the best strikers and they really need to practise a lot so it comes more easily to them in a game.'

There was a slight pause, before she said, 'I used to be a striker.'

'You were?' Andy asked in delight. 'That's just perfect. Even if you can't play, you can take the striking practice, try to help them understand different tactics.'

He paused, then said, 'They're all misfits, Chelsea, my soccer players. A few of them are kids who badly need to lose weight and somehow getting them into something that would interest them seemed a better way than nagging them to diet. There are a couple of migrants and it's helping to settle them into the community, and two of the girls are recovering drug addicts so they're a bit tetchy at times.'

She smiled at him.

'Then a pregnant teenager should fit right in,' she said, and went back to the sink, to peel carrots this time.

As he, Ellie, and Chelsea sat down to a meal of lamb cutlets with mashed potatoes, peas and carrots a couple of hours later, he realised just how big an asset Chelsea could be. Not only by helping to prepare meals, but her cheerful chatter broke through the tension that usually reigned when he and Ellie were together.

Tonight they'd even laughed, teasing each other, remembering silly things, something that had become so rare it made his heart ache for what had been.

'You prepared the dinner, Chelsea, so I'll clear the table and stack the dishwasher,' Ellie announced.

'And I'll do the pots and pans,' Andy volunteered. 'Have you got something to do, something to read?' he asked Chelsea. 'Or feel free to use the television in the sitting room. Ellie might have explained there are only two channels but you might find something you'd like.'

'I'd rather read and there are plenty of books in the bedroom.'

She paused.

'Whose room was it?'

Andy thought for a moment.

'The three girls were always swapping rooms, but I think it was Eliza who ended up in that one. They were definitely her posters on the walls.'

Chelsea disappeared, but as he washed the few pots and pans, Ellie by his side, stacking the dishwasher, life felt almost normal—like the *old* normal…

He waited until she straightened then slid an arm around her shoulders.

'It might be good for us, having Chelsea here,' he said, then he couldn't resist drawing her closer and pressing a kiss, not on her lips but on her temple. He felt her tremble in response, then ease herself away.

But the dreamy little smile on her face told him she hadn't minded…

Ellie woke suddenly, startled by something she couldn't immediately place.

It had been a phone ringing. It must have been Andy's mobile because she could hear his voice now.

Had he changed his ring-tone that she hadn't immediately recognised it?

But why?

Maybe she was just confused.

She lay awake, aware a phone call to a doctor in the middle of the night wasn't a good thing.

The talking stopped, then she saw his shadowy figure appear in the doorway.

'Did it wake you?' he asked quietly.

'Habit,' she said. 'Do you need me?'

'Only every day!'

The words were barely there, nothing more than a jumble of sounds, and probably she'd imagined it for now he was talking again. Asking about someone, a patient apparently...

'Yes, Madeleine's one of my patients,' she said, catching up with the conversation although the 'only every day' words still hovered in her head.

And heart...

'Has something happened to her?'

'Accident out on the Wyndham Road,' Andy said, pulling on the clothes he must have carried as far as the doorway. 'I don't suppose—'

'You need me to come? Why didn't you say so?'

Ellie was out of bed and pulling on the clean clothes she'd left out on a chair for the morning.

More mumbling from Andy—what was wrong with the man?

But her own guilt was more urgent now than

whatever was worrying Andy. For weeks she'd been seeing Madeleine for what had seemed like minor and confusing symptoms—aches and pains, tiredness, night cramps.

Ellie had seen her so often without pinning down a diagnosis that thoughts of Munchausen's syndrome had flashed across her mind, but the symptoms had never seemed serious enough. Not that she knew much about the syndrome.

'She *has* been complaining of dizzy spells lately. Where is she?'

'Apparently, she ran into a tree. Someone saw the accident and phoned the ambulance so she should be at the hospital by now.'

'I'll come with you,' Ellie said, and was startled when Andy gave her a hug as he thanked her.

Although after that kiss, mild though it had been…

She followed him out to the car—rarely used as the hospital was only three blocks away—wondering what was going on. Could Andy also feel that they could make their way back together as they'd first begun their courtship?

With touches, shared glances, even a little kiss…

But if Andy was happy to have her company, Madeleine seemed less so.

'You didn't have to come,' she told Ellie as Andy completed the handover from the ambulance personnel.

'You're my patient,' Ellie said, hoping she sounded more sympathetic than she felt. 'I was worried about you.'

'Well, I told you I was having dizzy spells and what did you do?'

Quite a few investigations, Ellie would have liked to remind her, but this was hardly the time.

Though Madeleine seemed only a little the worse for wear. A graze on her forehead was the only visible injury.

'Did your airbag deploy?' Ellie asked.

'No, it didn't!' her patient snapped. 'The ambulance people insisted on bringing me here and calling Andy,' she said, 'although I'm really perfectly okay.'

'Best we keep you under observation for the night,' Andy said. 'I'll do a scan of your head to make sure there's no internal damage, and nurses will check you every two hours. You won't get much sleep as they have to wake you, as well as check your blood pressure and temperature.'

'You'll be here, won't you?' Madeleine asked. 'Just in case anything goes wrong?'

'I *could* stay,' Andy said, and Ellie raised her eyebrows. The woman was playing him—surely he could see that!

She stomped out of the cubicle, then heard Andy leave behind her.

'There's no way you need to be up here all night just to hold that woman's hand,' Ellie told him.

He looked slightly startled.

'I'll do an X-ray and a scan first and take it from there,' he said.

'It's a graze!' Ellie reminded him. 'She didn't hit the tree hard enough for the airbag to deploy.'

'But there could have been whiplash,' he said.

'Believe me, there will be!' Ellie muttered. 'That woman comes to see me at least three times a week and I swear she's the healthiest patient I've ever seen.'

Andy looked puzzled.

'But if you don't like her, why did you come up to the hospital with me?'

She looked into the dark eyes she knew so well.

'I don't dislike her, and anyway, you asked me to,' she reminded him, which seemed to make him even more puzzled.

'I'll walk home,' she said, desperate to get away from the hospital and Madeleine Courtney, but most desperately needing distance between herself and Andy—distance so she could think…

# CHAPTER FOUR

'I MIGHT JUST as well have stayed with you at the hospital for all the sleep I got,' Ellie grumbled as she bumped into Andy in the en suite bathroom next morning.

A freshly showered and shaved Andy. The scent of his familiar aftershave filling her with a sense of longing.

'I slept like a log in a spare room at the hospital,' he said cheerfully. 'The nurses knew to wake me if Madeleine's condition showed any signs of deterioration, but there was really nothing wrong with her. I saw from her file she'd been seeing you quite often—is there something specific, do you think?'

'Not that I and a battery of tests can find,' Ellie muttered, so distracted by her husband's proximity she could barely think straight.

Had Andy picked up on a terseness in her voice that he said, 'Well, she's been very helpful to me with the soccer teams.'

Ellie bit back the comment, *I'm sure she has*, which she'd have liked to utter, and backed out of the room. Maybe if she took a few deep breaths, the room would be vacant by the time she returned.

And had Andy always worn aftershave to work?

She didn't think so, given the variety of allergies doctors were likely to encounter in their patients.

Was that jealousy coiled like a serpent in her stomach? And, if it was, did she have any right to be jealous? Whatever she and Andy had, it was hardly a marriage in the real sense of the word.

Not now. Not any more…

*But I love him*, a voice whispered in her heart, which she instantly dismissed as nonsense.

She was tired. She needed to have a shower, a quick breakfast, and get back to work. She must remember to phone the high school about Chelsea getting in there, probably starting next week as there were only a couple of weeks left in the term…

And she should give their guest some money for paint. The previous night, after some prodding and prompting, Chelsea had admitted she'd like pale green walls, and both Andy and Ellie were happy to go along with that idea.

Ellie would need to buy brushes and rollers, a tin for the rollers, and some plastic spread-sheets.

By the time Ellie was showered and dressed the list she'd been using as a distraction had grown so long she knew it would be easier to take Chelsea to the hardware store in her lunch hour with the car, so they could bring everything back home.

The gods had decided to be kind to her. She reached the kitchen to grab some breakfast, to find it was Andy-free.

'He only came home for a shower and some fresh clothes,' Chelsea explained to Ellie. 'He said he'd had a patient in a road crash last night so I suppose he was up all night.'

There was no point in disabusing Chelsea of that notion, no reason why she should be caught up in their marital stalemate…

Much better to concentrate on pale green walls.

'I should be home by twelve-thirty,' she told Chelsea. 'If you grab something to eat before then, we'll go down town and get what you need for decorating your room. Have you done any painting?'

Chelsea beamed at her.

'Dad taught me. He said girls should be useful around the house, so when I turned ten I got to choose what colour I wanted my room, and he showed me how to paint it.'

*Not a totally absent father, then*, Ellie thought.

Ellie's morning passed smoothly, although again, as she listened to some of her elderly male patients, she wondered what could be done to occupy their time.

Chelsea picked up on it when they were in the hardware store, where several older men were poking around, fiddling with bolts and nuts, lifting things and putting them back, looking, more than shopping.

'Don't they have anything to do?' she asked.

'Not a lot,' Ellie told her honestly.

'They need a Men's Shed,' Chelsea said, echoing what had only been a nebulous thought in Ellie's mind.

'What do you know about Men's Sheds?' she asked, and Chelsea smiled.

'My gramps—Mum's dad—belongs to one. They get old bicycles and old plastic chairs, sometimes from hotels, and turn them into wheelchairs that they send off to Africa and the Pacific Islands—anywhere people can't afford fancy wheelchairs.'

'Does your gramps still do it?' Ellie asked, excited by the idea.

'Sure.'

'And would he send you instructions on how to do it?'

'I'm sure he would.

'Well, let's phone and ask him—you can use our phone.'

'I'll write to him,' Chelsea replied, 'because I'll have to explain why I'm here and not at home. He'll probably assume Mum arranged it before she went away.'

They collected all they needed, Chelsea insisting on paying with her credit card, and headed home, seeing more elderly men sitting on a bench outside the supermarket.

The Men's Shed idea was growing, but how many old bicycles and plastic chairs could they source in Maytown?

'Plenty!' Andy said, when they were discussing the idea over dinner. 'I bet you've never had a good look in our garden shed. I'd say there'd be half a dozen in there. We all had bikes as kids, and when we outgrew the small ones, we got bigger ones, or for the girls just fancier ones. The old ones always ended up in the shed—just in case we might need them later, or could give them to a friend or a cousin.'

'And I suppose the garden shed might also house any number of old plastic chairs?' Ellie said, with only a slight edge of sarcasm.

'Well, if you mean those white ones that stack easily, then yes, there'd be some. We always needed extra chairs when relatives came for Christmas, and Mum and Dad never threw anything away. You never know when it might come in handy, that's Mum's favourite saying.'

Ellie could only shake her head, but Chelsea was all for going down to explore the garden shed immediately.

'Not at night, my girl,' Andy said firmly. 'The place hasn't been opened for months and who knows what snake might have made his home in there. I'll go down in the morning and open the doors and bang the sides a bit so any nasties lurking in there will have time to get out before we explore.'

'Oh, well,' Chelsea said, 'I have to email Gramps anyway, so I'll do that now.'

'Just as soon as we've cleaned up after dinner,' Ellie reminded her, and Chelsea leapt to her feet and began to clear the table, Andy deciding that with two people already cleaning up, he could get on the internet and investigate wheelchairs made from old bicycles. The idea intrigued him, although how they did it, he couldn't imagine.

He paused in the doorway, looking back at Ellie, who was stacking the dishwasher.

'This Men's Shed is a good idea,' he said. 'I'll phone Ray at the pub about old plastic chairs.'

Ellie smiled at him, feeling that this was as close to normal as they'd been for many, many months.

Could working together on a project like this heal the breach between them?

Or was it simply because they had a third person around—someone with her own problems—that the tension between herself and Andy seemed to have eased somewhat?

Andy had barely left the room when his phone rang.

It was Madeleine Courtney, who was feeling faint and dizzy, and wondering if it could be delayed concussion.

'Are you at the hospital?' he asked.

'No, I didn't like to drive,' came the weak and plaintive reply.

'Then I'll let Ellie know and she'll come to you,' Andy said. 'She's your GP.'

He could hear Madeleine suggesting he'd be better, but he stopped the conversation, returning to the kitchen where Ellie was on her own, doing the last of the wiping down of the benches.

'It's Madeleine Courtney,' he said, aware that

the name had come out as a growl. 'She thinks she might have delayed concussion.'

'She's at home?' Ellie asked, and he nodded.

'I'll go,' Ellie told him. 'But if there's any doubt at all she should be in hospital, shouldn't she?'

The frown on her face told him more than the words.

'*Is* there something wrong with her?' he asked.

'Apart from a maybe concussion that had her phoning you rather than me?' Ellie muttered. 'I'm beginning to think she feels I've failed her. There's nothing I can find—or have found so far—but you know full well that we do miss things.'

She sighed, then gave a little shrug.

'I'll go and see her and if I'm worried I'll drive her to the hospital myself and ask the staff to do hourly obs. And maybe if she's in hospital you can run more tests on her to see if I've missed something. Her symptoms are so vague, and change from pains in the abdomen to pains in her shoulders, to general tiredness, fuzzy concentration and, really, there's something new each visit. I've done tests for a thyroid condition—both hyper and hypo—but nothing's come back positive.'

'Could it be some kind of lupus, do you think?'

'I really don't know. None of the blood tests showed indications it could be that, and her urine analysis was clear, but I'll keep looking.'

She sighed.

'Sometimes I wonder if she's just homesick, but she always talks quite happily about the school and all she's doing.'

Ellie sounded so depressed by the thought Andy wanted to hug her.

Damn it all, why shouldn't he?

He gathered her in his arms, holding her close.

'We'll work it out, I promise,' he said, then bent and kissed her, a feather brush, nothing more, on the lips.

Startled blue eyes looked into his as Ellie shuffled back, turning towards the door, already on her way…

Escaping?

'I'll get her to the hospital. Should I ask for half-hourly obs? Quarter-hourly?'

She paused, looking up at him, doubt clouding her eyes.

Andy shrugged, then he remembered the light-hearted dinner they'd shared, the hug, the almost-not-there kiss, and swore softly.

'No, damn it all! Why should either of us be running all over town after her? I'll phone the ambulance to pick her up, and ask someone to call me as soon as she's settled, then I'll pop up and see her there. If there's any doubt, I can repeat the X-rays and scans we've already done, just in case there's something we've missed.'

'Are you sure? I'm happy to go.'

'No, let's get her to hospital, then tomorrow, when we've both had a good night's sleep, we can sit down with your notes and have a think about what the symptoms could indicate.'

'You've got soccer tomorrow,' she reminded him, and he was surprised she'd remembered.

'We'll do it after soccer.'

Andy phoned the ambulance and then the hospital, assuring them he'd be up to have a look at Madeleine, and ordering the X-rays of her head and neck.

He was about to leave when he thought of something, tapping on Ellie's door before going in. She'd had a shower and was wrapped in a towel, her wet hair hanging straight down by her face.

How could he not remember times he'd have ripped off that towel and tumbled them both onto the bed? His voice was croaky when he said, 'If we can't find anything maybe we should send her to the city. They have the facilities—not to mention the budget—to run tests we couldn't attempt.'

Ellie smiled at him, exacerbating all the reactions going on in his body.

'You'd have to hope they find something—some of those tests cost a mint—and maybe it *is* nothing more than hypochondria.'

Andy didn't respond but Ellie knew he would be grumbling and growling under his breath.

Could it be hypochondria? Ellie wondered when Andy left, fixing her mind on her patient to try to still the excitement Andy's kiss earlier had left in its wake.

Unfortunately, there was a strong possibility there *was* something wrong with Madeleine, in which case both she and Andy would regret it if they didn't do all they could for her.

Andy wandered off, probably to walk up to the hospital so he could meet the ambulance when it arrived.

Ellie shed her towel and pulled on pyjamas, glancing with a little regret at the pretty lingerie that occupied the other end of the drawer.

She laughed at her own stupidity. As if seducing her husband in sexy night attire could mend a marriage that harsh and hurtful words had ripped apart.

Ripped…

It was the strange word—describing well the seismic shift between them—that made her look through the more attractive negligees, down to the bottom of the pile where a dark blue, lacy, thigh-length piece of apparel still showed clearly that *it* had been ripped apart.

By passion, excitement, and a fiery need that could not be delayed…

And for a moment, holding it, she closed her eyes and remembered, awakening memories in her body as well, so she ached for Andy in a way she hadn't since they'd split apart…

*Could* they heal the rift—cross the abyss between them?

Had she been so wrapped up in her own pain she'd not considered his?

If so, wasn't it up to her to at least try to sort things out?

But where to start?

Determinedly putting aside such thoughts, she went in search of Chelsea. The teenager appeared to be coping well—talking enthusiastically about school and soccer—but the future of the child she would produce had hardly been mentioned.

Might she want to talk more about it?

And if so, should Ellie bring it up?

Doing so now, it would be as a friend. Or would it be better to do it at an appointment, as a doctor?

'Come and see,' Chelsea called to her as she dithered on the veranda, and Ellie entered the room, the soft green walls making it seem bigger somehow.

'Do you like it?' Chelsea asked, her face alight with so much joy Ellie could hardly find fault.

Not that she did.

'It looks great,' she said. 'But you don't want to sleep with the paint fumes tonight, so take one of the other rooms, then, in the morning, Andy will give us a hand to move the furniture back in. Unless…'

She hesitated.

'You might like to paint the furniture as well. I'd say the bed and desk and dressing table were painted white years ago, but they might look shabby in here now. There's probably white paint in the shed. What do you think?'

Chelsea settled on the bottom rung of the ladder she'd been using for the top of the high walls. She studied Ellie for a while before she spoke.

'Are you this kind to all the strays who land on your doorstep?' she asked softly, her eyes now bright with tears.

'Not *all* of them,' Ellie said gently. 'Only ones who know how to paint, and can help Andy with his soccer team, and bring a lot of pleasure to our house with your smile and enthusiasm—especially your smile!'

She went to squat beside Chelsea as the tears that had shone in her eyes now trickled down her cheeks.

'Besides,' she said, hugging the girl, 'you're family and if there's one thing Andy and I feel very strongly about, it's family.'

Her heart felt heavy as she said the words, but in spite of all that had happened, she knew family *was* important to them both.

'We'll do whatever we can to keep you safe and comfortable,' she said, 'and you can talk to either one of us about anything at all, but in the end everyone has to take responsibility for his or her own life, and that includes their own happiness.'

'And my baby?' The words came out as a quavery whisper. 'What should I do about that?'

Ellie hugged her.

'Let's wait and see,' she said. 'There's plenty of time to think about what you want both for yourself and for the baby. Have you thought much about it?'

She felt Chelsea nod against her chest.

'Only every day!' the girl whispered. 'It's my responsibility, isn't it, but what kind of life can I give a baby?'

She raised her head to look directly at Ellie, and added, 'But can I just give it away? As if it were an old bicycle I don't need any more? I'm not sure I could do that. Then I think that plenty of adopted babies grow up happy and contented and they bring joy to their new parents, so would I be selfish not letting it be adopted? Not giving the joy of a baby to someone who can't have one?'

The words cut into Ellie's heart. How easy would it be—

*No!* She mustn't think that.

Thrusting the thought away, Ellie drew Chelsea into her arms again, dropping a kiss on the top of her head.

'There's a lot to think about but nothing has to be decided right now. Any time you want to talk about it, Andy and I are here to listen. But right now you've had a busy and probably exhausting day, so why don't you have a shower and go to bed? Remember you're helping Andy with his soccer team tomorrow.'

Andy had arrived at the hospital as the ambulance pulled in. He greeted Madeleine and walked beside her as the ambulance men wheeled her into the observation room in the hospital's small Emergency Department. Her health records were already up on the screen and he checked the tests Ellie had previously ordered, and read the results.

As she had said, there was nothing to indicate any underlying cause for Madeleine's various symptoms, but there was still the possibility of delayed concussion from the accident.

He watched as the nurse on duty hooked Madeleine up to the monitor and wrapped a blood-pressure cuff on her arm.

'This will drive you nuts,' the nurse said cheerfully. 'It inflates every hour to record your BP, and it's usually just as you're dropping off to sleep. But we have to know what your body's doing, and if there's any major change then bells and whistles will let us know you need attention.'

'Bells and whistles?' Madeleine said faintly, perhaps regretting her decision to phone a doctor.

'More like a loud beeping noise,' Andy told her, as the nurse dashed off to answer a loud beeping noise elsewhere. 'Are you in any pain?'

'Well, my neck and shoulders ache, but they often ache, and I took some paracetamol for my headache about an hour ago, but the pain's not so bad. I'm used to it. It's the dizzy feeling I've got that worried me.'

Andy felt her head, his fingers seeking any

lump he might have missed earlier, but the only sign that there'd been an accident was a slight graze and a tiny bit of swelling on her forehead.

He checked Madeleine's eyes but both pupils reacted evenly to the light, and asked her some basic questions to test for confusion, but nothing obvious showed up.

'Try to get some sleep,' he said, and went back to the desk to go through Madeleine's file again.

Ellie arrived as he was checking the X-rays they'd done earlier.

'You'll be busy tomorrow and I thought we could go through her history together,' she said.

He smelt the bath soap she'd used, and felt her freshness against his shoulder, her head so close to his that a single turn of his head and he could kiss her again…

But he wouldn't. They were at work.

'I'm checking the X-rays—' as if she couldn't tell '—wondering if I've missed a hairline fracture anywhere.'

'There's nothing I can see. Are there scans as well?' Ellie asked.

But the scans showed Andy hadn't missed a bleed at the back of the brain from a contra coup injury. Ellie used a light beam to search every section of the brain.

Finding nothing, Andy shook his head, sorry Ellie had straightened up as he'd enjoyed her closeness.

'Well, all that's left is to go back through her medical history.'

Thanks to a government initiative, more than seven million people now had their health records available to doctors and hospitals all over Australia. Would Madeleine's be online?

It was, and this time Ellie squeezed onto the chair beside him. It was uncomfortable but, oh, so, comforting!

'As you can see,' Ellie said, 'she rarely visited her GP back in Sydney. She's had the usual flu vaccinations, scripts for oral contraceptives and apart from a bad case of laryngitis she suffered two years back, she's had no real health issues.'

'Until she came to Maytown,' Andy pointed out.

Ellie leaned over his shoulder again, resting her hands on the desk beside the keyboard.

She was so close he could feel the contours of her body against his back and was reminded of how they'd slept, spooned together.

'You can see everything seems trivial,' Ellie said, using the mouse to scroll down the visit list. 'Sore hip, bad neck, not sleeping, feeling of exhaustion even when she did sleep…'

But when Andy saw the battery of tests Ellie

had run, he knew she was taking Madeleine seriously. He read on through the file, Ellie pulling up a chair and sitting beside him now.

Some months ago she had prescribed Madeleine a mild anti-depressant, which was good thinking when nothing could be pinned down clinically, but apparently the tablets had made Madeleine feel nauseous and hadn't improved her aches and pains.

An anti-anxiety tablet had had much the same effect, with no positive outcome.

Frustrated by the lack of clinical evidence, Andy went back to see his patient, who was now sleeping even as the blood-pressure cuff inflated on her arm.

If the symptoms had only begun when she'd come to the high school here in Maytown, maybe Ellie was right about her problem being psychological.

'Was she unhappy about the transfer?' Andy asked his wife, as she, too, peered down at the sleeping patient. 'Could she just be miserable?'

He could practically hear Ellie thinking.

'We *have* talked about it,' she said at last. 'It was easy to bring up because I'm a newcomer to Maytown myself, but she's always responded enthusiastically: about the town, the school, everything…'

'You're starting to sound uncertain,' he said,

and saw the little frown line between Ellie's grey-blue eyes—a line she tried to rub away whenever she was aware of it.

Like now…

'She might have been too positive about it all,' she eventually admitted. 'But, honestly, Andy, I think whatever she has is real. I've been thinking fibromyalgia but that's such a hard thing to pin down and I've never known a patient with it, so I've no comparison I can make.'

'It's a good thought, though. That or some other auto-immune problem,' Andy told her. 'And having something like that, which *is* difficult to diagnose, could make her more anxious about possible concussion.'

'Because she knows there's something wrong with her but if the doctors can't find what it is, could they also miss something else?'

Andy put his arm around Ellie's shoulders, thinking of the times when they'd been studying or working together, and their minds had been so aligned they could finish each other's thoughts.

How could something that had been so strong—so right in every way—break down the way their marriage had? How had grief pushed them apart when it should have drawn them closer together? Had he been wrong, not sharing his feelings at the time, not wanting to burden her with more angst?

He pushed the thoughts away, and focussed on his patient. His go-to strategy since the break-up…

'I think we should leave it for another day,' he said. 'I'll stay a while in case she wakes with more confusion, but I'll let you go.'

Andy suggested it because it had been a long day and he knew Ellie would be tired, but thoughts prompted by the words 'I'll let you go' kept running through his head.

He walked back into the ward where Madeleine was still sleeping.

He *had* let Ellie go—quite literally—when the pain of the loss of their baby had been so overwhelming, so all-encompassing for him, he'd felt he hadn't been able to help her with *her* grief and despair.

*Or* done enough to get through the layers of protection she'd wrapped around her own grief.

So guilt had been added to his certain knowledge that he could never go through that anguish again—never face the hope and elation, the despair and pain…

'No, no, no!' he'd shouted when she'd suggested one last round of IVF. 'No more, not now, not ever.'

Then he'd killed any chance of redemption

with his bitter, caustic words: 'If this marriage needs a baby to make it complete, then it can't be much of a marriage.'

# CHAPTER FIVE

SATURDAY DAWNED AND Madeleine insisted she was feeling much better, so she was the first person Ellie saw when the soccer players started gathering on the side veranda. Madeleine looked fit enough, although she appeared to be limping. Had she bumped one of her legs in the car accident, mild though it had been?

Ellie introduced Chelsea to those players she'd met as patients, and, after leaving an ice-box full of cold drinks in a shady part of their 'clubhouse', she departed.

But with plenty of open doors leading out that way, she was able to observe what was going on without actually spying.

Her thoughts inevitably led to her and Andy. Though things were better between them, they were still living apart. Perhaps she and Andy should formalise their separation—people could be separated and continue living in the same house.

It wasn't that she wanted to be with anyone else, but Andy might… Despite the kiss, he'd made no further moves, so maybe he didn't want to be with her.

But that thought, and the one that followed it—separation usually led to divorce—made her feel cold all over.

*Could* she live without Andy?

It was impossible even to envisage such a thing. Just imagining it filled her with a deep, primeval pain. Losing Andy would be like losing part of herself…

But *if* he wanted his freedom, surely she should—

*No!*

A future without Andy was like looking into a bottomless pit or a black hole. It was emptiness, nothingness, a space she didn't want to inhabit…

It was better to think about other things, like the Men's Shed. They'd need a shed, of course, but from what she'd seen, sheds were common in this country town, and there was an old School of Arts building—very dilapidated, but perhaps their first project could be renovating it.

For which they'd need money.

Maybe they could ask one of the service clubs in town to help them raise funds. Ellie had already volunteered to bake cupcakes on the last Friday of each month for a stall raising money for soccer uniforms.

But the Men's Shed would need more money than a monthly cake stall could provide.

Who among her patients might belong to a service club?

Madeleine's arrival in the kitchen stopped further thought.

'I didn't think I hurt anything in the accident,' she said, with no hint of apology for disturbing Ellie at the weekend. 'But it's my knee. It was fine yesterday but this morning, after I left the hospital it felt a bit swollen and sore, and now it's getting worse, and I feel really unwell.'

She did look ill, so Ellie led her into one of the spare bedrooms and asked her to lie down.

The knee was red and inflamed but there was no hint of a scratch or graze that could have led to infection.

Was it because none of the other areas of pain Madeleine had complained of—the neck and shoulders—had been likely to swell, that Ellie had leaned more towards fibromyalgia than lupus? Joint pain and swelling definitely pointed to lupus.

'I know it's painful, but it might mean that we can pin down what's wrong with you and give you a proper diagnosis that fits all your symptoms,' Ellie told her. 'There's a strong possibility that it could be lupus.'

'Is it curable?' Madeleine asked.

'Unfortunately not,' Ellie told her. 'But a short course of corticosteroids will ease the pain and the inflammation in your knee. If it *is* lupus, your immune system is attacking you. All your joints have small fluid sacs, bursae, in them to protect the bones and their attached muscles and tendons as you move. Your immune system is attacking that fluid in your knee. The tablets will help you now, but we'll have to look at a longer-term solution to keep you as symptom free as possible.'

Madeleine frowned at her.

'So it's not going to go away like measles or something else contagious?'

Ellie shook her head.

'Are you going back to the city for the Christmas holidays?' she asked Madeleine.

'Yes, I'm going down to stay with my parents in Sydney.'

'Then I'd like you to see a specialist in clinical immunology while you're down there. I can make the appointment for you, because you're more likely to get in to see someone at short notice if a doctor asks. I can do most of the tests so he or she will have all the results before your visit.'

'But if you do the tests and have the results, why can't you treat me?'

Ellie sighed.

'I could, but a specialist will be able to do more for you, and make more appropriate suggestions about your treatment long term. Then I can follow up on it. There are drugs that can help when you have a flare-up like your knee, some drugs that can suppress your immune system, which might provide a little protection, and drugs like anti-malaria drugs that affect the immune system, but all these drugs have side-effects. If we have a specialist giving an overview of your treatment, we'll be getting advice about new treatments and suggestions when things don't seem to be working.'

'Will it kill me?'

Ellie shook her head.

'It shouldn't, but it can affect your kidneys and your liver, neither of which you want to damage. A specialist will advise on the best way to protect and watch over them.'

She was silent for a moment, dredging up all she knew about the disease.

'A lot of people go for long periods with no problems, beyond an occasional flare-up like your knee. They take non-steroidal anti-inflammatories when they have aches and pains, and cortisone when there's a painful attack like you're having now. I've some tablets in the surgery I'll give you to take now as any steroids are best taken in the morning—'

'So I'm not totally hyper at bedtime,' Madeleine said, and Ellie smiled.

'Exactly,' she said. 'I'll give you a script for more, but they are things you can't stay on long term because of side effects, but you also can't come off them suddenly. You should take one full tablet for four days, then a half for four days, then, believe it or not, a quarter for four days, then stop until you get another bad attack. You rest here while I slip down to the surgery.'

And to her surprise, Madeleine reached out and touched her on the arm.

'Thank you,' she said. 'I know I've been a nuisance, but I've always been so healthy and all the aches and pains took me unawares.'

Ellie grinned at her.

'Me, too,' she said. 'And I'm sorry we didn't get it worked out sooner, but I think we're onto it now.'

She hurried down the stairs, mentally listing all the tests she'd want to repeat and the new ones she'd have to order before Madeleine saw the specialist.

Andy had noticed Madeleine limp away from the group on the veranda, but he was far too busy trying to get his squad in order for some warm-up drills to wonder what was wrong with her now.

It didn't seem to matter how far and how fast modern medicine progressed, something new was always appearing, although the more he'd thought about Madeleine's file, the more he'd wondered about lupus.

Ellie had written 'query lupus' early in her contact with Madeleine, but the normal tests like a full blood count, erythrocyte sedimentation rate, and urinalysis hadn't shown anything abnormal. There were more tests, but all testing was expensive, so both hospital doctors and GPs tried to keep to the budgetary restraints imposed on them.

Practice over—the old tennis court had proved its worth—he set the older boys to tend the barbecue and left Chelsea to organise slicing onions and buttering bread. Sausage and onions in a slice of bread was standard fare for lunch before a game, while the icebox contained various kinds of water—plain and lightly fruit flavoured, carbonated and still.

'This is a far better idea than a barbecue in the park,' Madeleine said, joining them on the veranda, her right knee bandaged. 'You can keep them all in one place, not drifting anywhere they fancy. Do we walk down to the field?'

Andy grinned at her.

'When we've got the school bus to take us? No, we'll conserve all our energy for the game. Woonunga has two teams but as it's just a trial before the start of the season in the New Year, we'll just play one game, swapping the players at half-time. We haven't got two full teams so some kids will have to play a bit longer but we'll sort it out.'

Chelsea appeared at Ellie's side as she sat at the kitchen table, writing lists of people she wanted to contact about the Men's Shed, either for advice, donations, or help.

'It's their first real game against opposition, and Andy's got the school bus to take us down.'

Ellie looked at her young boarder, in shorts, a loose shirt and, incongruously, football boots.

'Someone had a spare pair. And I won't join the game because Andy checked and I can't play after the first trimester. I just wanted to feel I was part of it,' Chelsea explained. Then she looked up at Ellie.

'Do come,' she said, and Ellie knew she couldn't resist.

She started on the sideline, standing next to Andy, feeling the tension in his body as his team took to the field for their first game against an opposition.

She slipped her hand into his and squeezed his fingers.

'They'll be fine,' she said. 'And when all's said and done, it's just a game.'

He gave her a horrified look,

*'Just a game?'* he echoed, then grinned and returned the pressure of her fingers.

But as soon as the game began, he was racing up and down the sideline, yelling orders. Other people joined her, people she knew as patients, or had met around the village.

'It's a damn good thing for the kids that Andy's started this,' the butcher told her, and the warmth of pride spread through her body.

To Ellie's surprise, the Maytown team seemed to be doing well. The young person in charge of the score was a bit erratic, but Ellie knew they'd definitely scored two goals to Woonunga's one.

But what really surprised her was the support—not only from the parents of participants yelling encouragement from the sidelines but half the town seemed to be there.

'If we go over there to play them when the season begins in earnest in the New Year, I reckon I can get a busload of supporters,' the butcher said.

The game finally finished, a three-all draw, and one of the local service clubs put on a barbecue for the players and supporters.

It was an opportunity for Ellie to mention the Men's Shed idea to one of the women there.

'Oh, bless you for the wheelchair idea,' the woman said. 'A group of us have been discussing getting something started but they need a goal, something to focus on. They don't want to be learning wood-turning or polishing stones—they need a project they'll really believe in. You leave it with me now, I'll get my husband onto it.'

Ellie felt an arm slide around her waist, and Andy was there.

'Are you lobbying these people for support for your Men's Shed?' he asked, smiling at the group who'd now gathered around Ellie.

'Just talking,' Ellie replied, through lips that were suddenly dry, while her knees were definitely wobbly.

But the women were all talking to Andy now, congratulating him on setting up the soccer team, explaining how so many of the kids had too much time on their hands in summer when their normal Rugby League football season was over.

There were offers of help with fundraising for uniforms and maybe setting up a regular canteen at matches.

'With coffee,' another woman said. 'I could have murdered a cup of coffee at half-time.'

Realising this was Andy's show, Ellie was about to step away, but Andy's hand in the small of her back stopped her moving.

Stay, that touch seemed to say. Stay and share the talk with me.

Excitement built within her. They'd been studying together when their first romance had begun, and now they were kind of working together, occasionally at the hospital *and* on projects like the soccer teams and Men's Shed. Andy might like to get involved with that, too, while she could do more to help with the soccer team.

They walked home, just the two of them, Chelsea having gone to look at old bicycles one member of the soccer team knew of, and Madeleine having left early to go home and rest her knee.

Ellie could feel Andy's closeness through every nerve ending in her skin, could feel the warmth of his body next to hers.

Should she take his hand?

'If I change Joe—he's the rather overweight boy with ginger hair,' Andy announced, shocking Ellie from her wayward thoughts, 'from that back position to the forwards, then—'

No, she wouldn't take his hand.

She'd tune back into Andy's conversation instead, show an interest.

But their shoulders were touching, and his hand was right there, by hers.

'Then Rangi can go—'

Ellie gave up. There'd be other times they could hold hands and, really, wasn't being interested in what he was doing more important?

But did she have to be interested in the technical stuff? Wasn't organising cake stalls and raising money for uniforms just as important?

'Then Chelsea can give them some goal practice—'

'Only practice,' she reminded him as they turned in at their front gate. 'You'll work it out.'

Maybe they could sit down and have a drink together.

'Not if I don't write it all down. I can already see how it would make a difference.'

Frustrated that her imaginary scenario wasn't going to play out—at least not tonight—Ellie was about to say, *It's not the World Cup*, but she caught herself just in time.

That was the kind of sniping thing they'd said to each other too often in the past months. If she wanted to fix things—and she knew that she did—all that had to stop.

She must have sighed as she climbed the steps, for Andy turned to her, concern on his face.

'Are you okay? You probably shouldn't have

stayed for the whole game—it was hot out there in the sun. Come inside and I'll get you a cold drink.'

And he put his arm around her shoulders just as he would have in the old days, and led her into the kitchen, pulling out a chair for her then finding an open bottle of white wine and pouring her a glass.

'There,' he said. 'And let's not bother with dinner. I'll run up the road later and get a takeaway.'

After which he went to the far end of the long table where all his soccer papers were and began writing furiously, crossing out and shifting names as if his life depended on it.

How long since he'd touched Ellie—even for something as simple as an arm around her shoulders?

Yet that touch had stirred so much back to life, Andy knew they had to try again—to give it one last go to find a way back to each other, to the love they'd shared.

For a moment the flood of memories blanked everything from his mind. The pair of them as students, and the overwhelming joy of first love. Africa, where passionate, sweaty sex had helped them block out the horrors they'd seen during the day; where they'd kept going *because* they'd had each other. More recently their joyous arrival in Maytown, where they had hoped to grow from couple to family, sharing the delight of their new home, and their joy in their new baby.

There was far too much to throw away…

And if they did sort it out?

What next?

Was he willing to concede to one last attempt at IVF?

A huge black cloud immediately descended over his brain and pain tightened his chest.

How could he *not* have known how much losing a child—even an unborn one—would hurt? Yes, he'd been upset when the IVF attempts had failed, but more for Ellie's sake as he knew she'd somehow felt responsible.

But then it *had* worked, and he'd been talking to the bump in her stomach every day, often sharing silly things that had happened at work, sometimes just talking about the weather, the shining sun or sparkling stars.

They'd opted not to know the sex of their child, and somehow, when they'd lost it, finding out that it had been a boy had worsened his pain…

He forced himself to focus on the names on the paper in front of him, trying to remember all the changes he'd thought of for the soccer team as they had walked home.

Walking home with Ellie had felt so normal—so right—that he'd tried to keep his mind on soccer to stop himself from taking her hand.

If only he could get over the loss of the baby they *had* finally conceived.

Surely the pain should have grown less by now? Perhaps he should see a psychologist—take some time off and go down to the city. Better yet, find one on-line, someone he could talk to on a regular basis without it affecting his work…

Should they both have done that after the loss?

He tried to concentrate on soccer again.

If he shifted Joe—

But his mind had moved beyond football.

'I'll get the takeaway,' he said, standing up and closing his folder of soccer papers. 'Thai or Chinese?'

'Thai,' Ellie said, setting down her half-empty glass and standing up as well. 'I'll pop this in the fridge and come with you.'

He watched her walk to the fridge. Gold-blonde hair tangled by the breeze, slim waist and rounded hips as she bent to settle the wine. Then as she straightened and turned his heart leapt at the sight of his Ellie—her nose and cheeks pink from the sun, her grey-blue eyes smiling at him, her beautifully shaped lips echoing the smile…

His heart began behaving badly in his chest.

Could it be possible that she felt the same way—that *she* felt an easing of the tension between them?

'Well, are we going?' she said, and Andy realised he was standing by his chair, immobilised by the thoughts skittering around in his head, and the emotions churning in his body.

Hope—that was the main one. After all those weeks and weeks of nothingness, he'd felt the tug of a slender thread of hope…

Chelsea came home with news of bicycles, and talk about the Men's Shed dominated their meal.

'I'll leave you two to clean up,' Ellie said, when they'd finished. 'I need to do some research.'

She turned to Andy.

'With Madeleine's knee flaring up the way it did today, I'm back to thinking lupus so I'll do all the tests I can, and see if I can get her an appointment with a specialist when she's in Sydney for the holidays. Speaking of which…' she turned to Chelsea '…do you know when the school holidays begin?'

'Two weeks,' was Chelsea's prompt reply.

'Everyone in the team has been talking about them, where they're going, what they're going to do. Some of them have jobs lined up.'

'Then I'd better find a specialist soon, before everything stops for Christmas.'

Ellie left the room, left also an awareness of Andy's presence that she hadn't felt for months. They'd walked together, talked together, in a comfortable way—he'd even put his arm around her shoulders, drawn her close to his side. And whether it was Chelsea's presence in the house, or some force beyond her understanding, for whatever reason suddenly she could feel the knots of hard, hot resentment she'd felt towards him crumbling inside her.

Yet what she felt was more than hope.

Just as they'd fallen in love the first time, surely they could do it again? Could make their way back to each other, to togetherness, slowly and tentatively maybe—but eventually…

She grabbed the keys for the surgery and made her way down the stairs. Madeleine's file would have her Sydney address, and Ellie wanted to find her a specialist within reach of her parents' home, not in some far distant part of the sprawling city.

But when she unlocked and opened the door, she stepped back in dismay. While half the town had been at the football game, someone from the other half had broken into her surgery.

Broken glass that lay scattered across Maureen's desk in front of a window told her how they'd got in, but what had they taken?

Patient paper files were in locked cabinets, her work computer and Maureen's, and all the drugs, even non-dangerous ones, were locked in the safe.

She yelled up the stairs for Andy, although she could tell from the stillness that whoever had done this was long gone. But her knees were shaking, and she wasn't sure whether she should go in and check the safe or wait for the police.

'Oh, Ellie!' Andy whispered as he arrived by her side. Then he wrapped his arms around her and held her close.

'I think we phone Chris,' he said, speaking of the sergeant in charge of the local police station. 'Then wait and go in when he tells us it's okay.'

He held her steady with one hand so he could pull out his cellphone and speed-dialled the police station.

'He'll be here in ten minutes,' he told Ellie. 'Do you want to wait here or go up and lie down for a while?'

'I could get you a cup of tea,' Chelsea suggested from halfway down the stairs where she'd followed Andy.

Ellie shook her head.

'I'm okay. It was just the shock.'

She paused, her brain racing.

'Would they have gone upstairs? Should we check there? They wouldn't need to break in, there's always one of the doors open.'

'Best go and check,' Andy said. 'Chelsea can go with you, though I can't imagine anyone being so bold. Down here, with the garden all around, someone passing in the street wouldn't have noticed a stranger in the yard, but upstairs—even going up the steps—someone would have been sure to see them.'

Ellie knew he was talking to reassure her, but he was probably right. She joined Chelsea and they both went slowly through the house, checking easy-to-steal things like laptops, cellphones and other electronic paraphernalia.

But nothing appeared to be missing, although checking the drawers in Chelsea's room revealed just how little clothing the teenager had brought with her.

'This reminds me,' Ellie said to her as she slid the drawer shut, 'we should really go down to Croxton and get you some more clothes. It's the nearest decent-sized town and it's only about an hour's drive. What you managed to fit into your backpack won't last you through summer.'

'I don't want you having to fuss over me and drive me places,' Chelsea protested. 'I'm already so grateful to you both for taking me into your home. I can't let you do more.'

'Of course you can!' Ellie told her. 'But if it will make you feel any better, I love an excuse to go down to Croxton and poke around the shops there.'

Chelsea chuckled, but the sound of a vehicle pulling up had them both heading out onto the veranda.

'That's Chris—he's in charge, and the lad with him is—'

'Zeke!' Chelsea finished for her. 'He looked after me on the train and made sure no one bothered me. He's new in town, too, and he's staying in a hotel while he waits for a flat that will be empty when the school year ends. One of the teachers is leaving and Zeke's made arrangements to take it over.'

'You know more about what's going on in this town than I do,' Ellie told her. 'Shall we go down to hear what they say?'

There'd been a touch of hero-worship in Chelsea's tone as she'd spoken of Zeke, so it wouldn't do her any harm to meet up with him again.

And Ellie would check him out as well. He'd be nineteen or twenty if he was fresh out of the academy, and Chelsea wasn't always going to be pregnant, although she might always be in love with the boyfriend, Alex…

Ellie closed her eyes for a moment, thinking of the word 'always' and how she'd automatically attached it to love.

Because for her that's how it had seemed…

Chris greeted her with a smile and introduced Zeke, who immediately introduced Chelsea to his boss.

'It *has* happened before, in your parents' time, Andy,' Chris said. 'You'd think they'd learn there's nothing here to steal, although maybe someone in every generation has to have a go.'

He paused, then shrugged his shoulders.

'Come and see,' he said. 'There's plenty of glass. Are you both wearing something on your feet?'

Ellie looked down at her own and Chelsea's sandals and nodded.

They checked the window first. It was easy to see what had happened. It had been broken by a brick or rock, then a big enough hole bashed in it for the culprit to put his arm through and unlock the other side.

Smears of blood on the broken glass still in

the window suggested whoever had done it hadn't left unscathed.

As Chris led the way to the back storeroom, where things like paper towels and first-aid supplies were stored, Ellie stayed by the window, seeing where quite a lot of blood had pooled.

Anxious now, she followed the men and the blood spots on the floor, arriving in time to see Chris studying the big old safe in the corner of the room. Sooty black marks were all over the door.

'Kids, I reckon,' Chris said. 'Saw a movie where safe-crackers used a blowtorch to open an old safe and they've bought one of those little burners that some people use in the kitchen, or to solder maybe a broken link of a chain. All it had the power to do was make a mess, but it does point to it being someone quite young. I think even teenagers would know better.'

'Do you take fingerprints?' Ellie asked, although she was still thinking about the blood. 'Of young kids, I mean? Are you allowed to?'

Chris smiled at her. 'Young Zeke here, who's not long out of college, can probably quote the entire passage from the rule book on this, but, yes, we can take a child's fingerprints if we take him or her into custody and have both the child and the responsible adult's consent. There are rules about how long fingerprints, particularly of minors, are allowed to be kept, so we don't have file-drawers or even many digital records full of young offenders' fingerprints.'

'So, will you take fingerprints here?' Ellie asked, diverted from the blood by the working of the law.

'We will, and then we'll round up half a dozen young hooligans and give them a scare.'

'You might not need fingerprints to find our offender,' Ellie said. 'There was blood on the glass and it led into the storeroom, and look…'

She bent to pull a roll of blood-soaked cotton wool out from behind a cupboard.

'I'd say he's cut himself quite seriously. Wrapped the wound in his T-shirt so there's not much blood at the scene, but there's the occasional drip and now this.'

Andy reached her first, and felt the squelch of blood in the wool.

'He's bleeding badly,' he said. 'We need to find him.'

Chris reacted first to the urgency in Andy's voice.

'Zeke, get on to the local radio station and ask if they can put out a call for someone who suffered an injury that caused a lot of bleeding today. Tell them to get up to the hospital to be checked out. Ask parents to check their children to make sure they're not hiding an injury.

Then get on to regional TV and see if they can do a similar flash notice across the bottom of their screens.'

As Zeke hurried away, Chris sighed.

'Short of door-knocking the entire town, I don't see what else we can do.'

He thought for a few minutes, then added, 'Mind you, there are a few places I *can* door-knock.'

'You know the young rascals in town, then?' Ellie asked, and Chris nodded.

'In fact,' he said, 'I've been meaning to talk to Andy about them. Can you take a few younger ones into your soccer teams?'

'As many as you like,' Andy assured him. 'It would be good to have a team at every age level.'

'Then I'll give you five for free,' Chris joked. 'When should they turn up for practice?'

Andy thought for a moment.

'Tuesday afternoon. They can meet the older group and learn from them. Eventually we'll have separate sessions for the younger ones, but we can only do that if Ellie and I can work out a good job-sharing system.'

'Oh, you'll manage that, no problem,' Chris assured him. 'The way you two work so there's always someone on call for the hospital has impressed everyone in town. Not that your parents didn't do a good job, Andy, but the hospital had more staff then, and always two doctors.'

'Cloning one or other of us might help,' Ellie whispered, but Andy knew Chris was right. They *would* work it out. Even when their relationship had been at its worst, they'd managed their job-sharing efficiently and well, as if, in their work life, nothing had changed.

And thinking of work... 'I should get up to the hospital to wait for whoever was bleeding to come in. If it's a child, the parents might have bandaged the wound tightly enough to slow the blood flow, and not realised it's probably serious.'

'Or not reported it in case the child ended up in trouble,' Chris grumbled.

'I'll clean up here, then join you in case I'm needed,' Ellie offered.

Chelsea stepped forward.

'No, you go with Andy, I'll clean up here.'

'And I'll stay to help, if you can spare me, boss,' Zeke offered.

'Go for it,' Chris said, 'but both of you wear thick gloves—you can grab a couple of pairs from the car, Zeke—and get some more clothes and be very careful. That glass is old and extremely sharp. I don't want either of you joining the injured list.'

Ellie touched Andy lightly on the arm.

'I'll have a quick shower and then head to the hospital,' she said. 'I want to change my shoes because there's sure to be little bits of glass in the soles and I don't want to spread them wherever I walk.'

'Good thinking,' Andy said, smiling down at the practical, sensible woman he couldn't help loving in spite of all that lay between them. 'I'll change mine, too, then when I've got time I'll attack them with a wire brush. Yours and Chelsea's, too. Best to leave them on the veranda.'

His chest tightened, and inwardly he cursed himself that all he'd managed by way of conversation was safe glass removal from the soles of shoes.

There was so much he'd wanted to say, especially when she'd been holding his arm and looking up at him with a slight smile hovering around her lips.

Kissing her, which was what he *really* wanted to do, was impossible with everyone around, but even that desire had been absent for so long it had startled him.

'I'll see you upstairs,' he said, hoping his hurried exit didn't look as desperate as it felt.

She followed him up—had his thoughts drawn her to follow him?—and he held her arm to steady her as she slipped off her sandals.

And as she leaned into him, what else could he do but hold her, *and* kiss her, just as he'd envisaged it down in her surgery.

'Well, that was unexpected,' she said, her eyes dancing as she stepped, barefoot, away from her sandals. 'Something to do with the young love downstairs?'

'Young love downstairs?'

Had the kiss addled his brain?

'Didn't you see the way Chelsea blushed when Zeke got out of the car? There's a little bit of hero-worship going on there.'

'Nonsense, she only met him on the train.'

Ellie smiled.

'And you'd only met me that day in the refectory when you inveigled me into that corridor near the fire doors and kissed me almost senseless.'

'But I'd been looking at you all day in lectures.'

'As if that was an excuse,' Ellie teased, and for all the pain and anguish in between, the memory was enough to make him kiss her again, moving within seconds from a slow, exploratory kiss towards passion.

'You should be going,' Ellie whispered, but she didn't move out of his arms. In fact, this time it was she who kissed him.

'I've missed this so much,' she murmured

against his lips. 'How could we have let it all happen? Was my mentioning another IVF a kind of last straw for you?'

He held her closer, trying desperately to find the words he needed, but none seemed right, so he kissed her again.

*That* seemed right…

Until Chelsea appeared with a dustpan and brush, and wolf-whistled as she passed them.

'Cheeky brat!' Andy muttered, while Ellie laughed, but Andy's mind as he strode the couple of blocks through town was on Ellie more than the patient, who might or might not turn up.

He took a deep breath and refocussed on the patient.

What if he wasn't a local?

Could it be someone who'd come to the soccer but slipped away from his family or mates?

Could he have had a mate with him?

Might there be two patients?

An ambulance screaming into the hospital entrance ahead of Andy, suggested a lot of his questions had been answered.

'He's suffering from shock from a massive haemorrhage from an arm wound. The babysitter bandaged it and didn't realise it was still bleeding until the kid passed out.'

The ambo who'd leapt out on Andy's side

filled him in as he hurried to the back doors, where his partner was already wheeling out the patient.

The lad lying on the stretcher couldn't have been more than ten, and looked more like a ghost than a living being.

Andy didn't hesitate, hauling off his shoes as he walked through the doors and dropping them in a bin, grabbing the first nurse he encountered.

'Get on to my wife and tell her we need her ASAP,' he said. 'You'll find the number on the list above the triage desk.'

The stretcher was now through the door, and he helped steer it towards one of two resus rooms.

The ambulance monitor showed him the child's blood pressure was dangerously low, while his pulse was racing as his heart tried desperately to keep what little blood there *was* in his body pumping around the major organs.

'We put in a fluid line and have been giving him FFP, but we don't carry full blood,' the senior ambo told Andy.

'Neither do we—it just doesn't keep well—but we do have an O Group donor. And hopefully she's on her way here.'

Ellie walked in at that moment.

'Blood?' she guessed, and he nodded.

'I have to find the wound and do what I can to stem the flow,' he explained, 'so could you find one of the nurses with training to take yours? Just one bag to start off with, and stay lying down when it's filled. No heroics, understand?'

Ellie grinned at him, and walked out.

Andy released the tourniquet the ambulance men had put on the lad's upper right arm, and sighed when he saw the gash about five centimetres above the thumb and the spurt of blood when he released the pressure. The cut had gone deep enough to catch the radial artery.

He put a new pressure pad on it and wrapped it tightly, retightening the tourniquet while he found what he'd need for the repair.

In a child, the blood vessels were tiny, and in the city the repair would be a job for a micro-surgeon, but out here you did what you could. Particularly when there was no time to wait for the flying ambulance or even the flying doctor service.

Not that they'd have a micro-surgeon on board…

But in truth he liked the challenge to his skills that working in a fairly remote country hospital provided.

By the time he returned, the boy had been cleaned up and dressed in a hospital gown, ready to be transferred to their small operating theatre. In there, Andy had already set up the instruments he'd need, including the extremely expensive magnifying glasses most small hospitals didn't carry.

They'd been a present from Ellie when they'd moved up here.

Just in case, she'd said, and he'd had to use them several times, repairing delicate tissue.

And far from resting for a few minutes after donating her blood, it was Ellie who met him in Theatre, carrying the bag of blood she'd just had drained from her.

Back in the city, blood of the same type was mixed so recipients and donors rarely knew each other, but out here where fresh blood could take four hours to reach a patient if it had to be flown from the nearest city, having an O group donor—the universal group that mixed with all other blood—on hand was priceless and often could be life-saving.

Best of all, the blood had been collected in an approved blood collection bag, which held the appropriate amount of anti-coagulation chemicals, so it was safe to use immediately.

'Did you also bring a filter line?' he asked, unable to help grinning at her.

'Of course,' she said. 'And if you're doing a repair on a tricky little blood vessel you'll need help, so there's no point in my lying around resting.'

'We might need more blood,' he said, serious now.

'Well, I've got plenty more,' she assured him. 'Let's get this show on the road!'

# CHAPTER SIX

THE WOUND TO the radial artery was more a nick than a slice, and the uneven nature made it harder to repair as one wrong stitch could close off the artery completely.

Ellie watched as Andy used the finest gauge needles, and thread as fine as a spider's web, to delicately join the torn edges. He was so careful, so precise with his microscopic stitches that she wondered why he'd never considered a career in surgery.

But it would have meant a different life—mainly a city life—and Andy would have had to steer his registrar jobs in that direction almost as soon as they had become fully qualified.

But Africa had called to them. Films they'd seen of the colour and the vibrancy of the people had attracted them, and the knowledge that doctors were badly needed in many parts of the big continent had sent them in that direction.

They'd always seen their work in war-torn

African countries as a kind of gap year—an adventure as well as a chance to hone their skills in often impossible situations.

It had been good training, too, for work in remote areas back home—their ultimate aim—where you couldn't just phone a specialist already in the hospital to pop down to the ED to see a patient.

But when she had failed to get pregnant, they'd stayed on in the city, Andy keen to try IVF, more keen than she'd been in the beginning.

Deep down she knew he'd always had this dream of reliving his happy childhood by living and working in a country town, bringing up a horde of kids in a place where life was not too hectic.

They'd known the facts and figures about success rates with IVF, but like most hopeful couples had been sure theirs would be a lucky, first-time success. And when it hadn't been, trying again had seemed the natural thing to do, and so it had gone on…

Ellie pushed the thoughts away and concentrated on her job.

Acting as Andy's assistant, she had to keep the small wound clear of blood so he could see the artery at all times. When he'd tied his last knot, she held her breath, praying the stitches would hold when the tourniquet was released.

'Done!'

Andy gave a fist pump in triumph when no leakage appeared, then bent his head to piece together the wound itself.

'I'll need to repair the tendon,' he muttered under his breath, and seeing how the pale sinewy strand had shrunk back into itself, Ellie knew it would be nearly as difficult as fixing the artery.

Now her job was to ease one end of the cut tendon out from the mass of bone and muscle into which it had retreated, straining it towards the end Andy was pulling from the other side.

Using forceps, she finally held both sides together, while, working slowly and meticulously, Andy joined the two ends, then finally cleaned and closed the wound.

'BP's still low,' Andrea told them as she began to reverse the anaesthetic.

Ellie glanced at the bag of blood that hung by the boy's side.

Nearly empty.

'Do you want more or will you use FFP?' she asked Andy, aware that the hospital had a store of fresh frozen plasma.

'He's only small so FFP should do it,' Andy replied.

'Which means you get to keep your blood,' Andrea said, and Ellie smiled at her, aware they were all feeling relief that the operation was over, although the risk of infection would still be alive in everyone's mind.

'Do we know who he is?' Ellie asked, having missed the introductions while she was giving blood.

'Kid called Logan Grant,' Andrea explained. 'Dad's a miner. Mum hated the country—she lasted about a month after he took the job out here. The family had barely settled in before his wife headed back to the city.'

'Leaving Logan behind?'

'He's not the only one. There are three kids in his family and I know of at least one other family where it's happened, although in that one the wife went off with another miner, so it broke up two families. It's becoming the way we live these days, especially out here in the bush.'

*It's not the way I live*, Ellie was about to say, when she realised her situation wasn't so different. Okay, so she and Andy didn't have children to consider, but if they didn't have the tie of the house and the responsibilities of the positions they'd taken, would they both have stayed?

Would *she* have stayed?

More to the point, *could* she have left Andy?

Andrea was taking Logan through to the small recovery room, and Ellie and her thoughts followed Andy into the changing room.

'Would you have taken off back to the city if it wasn't for the house and job?' Andy asked, shocking her with the words that were echoes of her own thoughts.

'No!' she said, and only just stopped herself saying, *I love you*, because at the moment she wasn't sure how he'd take such a declaration.

Even after the kiss—kisses—they'd shared…

'Me neither,' he said, stripping off to reveal more of his strong, lean body than she'd seen for ages, before disappearing into the shower.

Ellie stripped off her theatre gear and used the second shower. They might have showered together many times at home, but never at the hospital—any hospital—although she did remember Andy suggesting it once when they'd been courting…

Were they courting now? Could starting over be called courting?

Wasn't that what she was…not exactly planning but working towards?

And was it in Andy's head as well? After all, not only had his arm been around her shoulders earlier, he had definitely kissed her on the veranda!

She could still feel the thrumming in her veins the second, harder kiss had caused…

If Chelsea hadn't suddenly appeared—

But she had, not that it stopped Ellie thinking of the kisses now, or hoping there'd be more before too long.

Andy was gone by the time she left the shower—the hospital had its own bore for water, so she sometimes sneaked a little extra shower time when she was there.

Would Andy still be at the hospital?

In with Logan perhaps…

Ellie made her way to the recovery room. There was no sign of Andy but Logan was just waking up, while his devastated teenage babysitter sat beside him.

'I need to get back to the girls,' she said. 'I left them with a neighbour but they'll play up with her and they'll be worried about Logan, but his father's not off shift.'

Ellie held up her hand to stop the flow of words.

'I'll stay with Logan,' she said, taking the child's hand in hers and giving it a little squeeze. 'That okay, Logan?' she asked, and the lad smiled.

The babysitter left and Ellie asked Logan about his family and school, pleased he was becoming more coherent as he answered.

'Am I in trouble?' It was his turn to ask a question.

'Maybe a little,' she said.

'Poor Dad,' he said. 'He'll think it's his fault, what with Mum going and all of that.'

'Why did you do it?' Ellie asked, sensing Logan was ready to talk.

'I'd seen the safe there when I had to get a tetanus shot last year and I thought there'd be money in it, and if I got some money then Mum might come back in time for Christmas.'

He made it sound so simple it made Ellie's heart ache.

'Love doesn't always work that way,' she said, gently stroking the boy's cheek. 'But it was a nice idea. And if you want to earn some money, I've got a garden that's getting far too overgrown for me to cope with. You could come over after school a couple of afternoons a week to pull out weeds and I'd be happy to pay you.'

Logan grinned at her.

'I'd like that,' he said, then slipped into sleep.

Would he remember this plan in the morning?

It didn't matter, Ellie could contact him.

But as her husband came in to check on his latest patient, she was wondering how love *did* work.

'Logan seems to be doing well,' Andy said,

his hand dropping to rest on Ellie's shoulder, sending messages—of love?—shooting along her nerves. 'His blood pressure is back to normal, and his heart rate down.'

'He was lucky the babysitter realised it was serious.'

'The main thing is we got him in time,' Andy reminded her. 'He's going to a ward now, so I'll walk you home.'

As they left the hospital, his hand brushed hers, and as the electricity from that casual touch shot through her body, she realised it hadn't been so casual a touch because now his fingers were tangled with hers.

They were hand in hand.

'Is it better if we don't talk?' he asked quietly. 'I think talking hurt us both too much.

'I've been thinking the same thing,' she whispered back, and his fingers tightened on hers—just briefly—signalling agreement, and something else; the beginning of a thaw...

Although hope seemed brittle—fragile—something one wrong word could break, the warmth of Andy's hand in hers, or hers in his, was sending so many messages leaping along Ellie's nerves that her brain was sizzling with visions of the future they had dreamed of.

Forget leaving Maytown at Christmas. *This*

was where she belonged—with Andy by her side…

Childless, but still with a future where they stood together, loved and loving.

'Could get Rangi to take the younger boys and be their coach. He knows more about soccer than I do and if Chelsea would be willing to help him, we'd have a new, younger team in no time.'

So much for sizzling visions!

Andy had probably taken her hand out of habit and didn't fully realise he was holding it.

Well, she had agreed it was better not to talk about their problems…

They'd reached the bottom of their stairs and Andy dropped her hand and peeled away.

'I want to open up the shed and bang around a bit so anything that's crawled in there to live might decide to leave.'

And with that he was gone.

Ellie was in bed by the time he returned, and when Andy slipped through the shared bathroom to look down at her, there was enough moonlight coming through the French doors to see she was deeply asleep.

It had been the nearly full moon that had made him think about kissing her earlier—not the first kisses but the later ones—when they'd walked home from the hospital together. He'd even picked out a spot, tucked against the old camellia at the bottom of the front steps.

The idea was so overwhelming he was sure Ellie could feel his emotion through his fingers, feel his body trembling slightly at the thought of it.

Then, like the idiot he was, he'd started worrying about pushing things too fast, about maybe her not wanting to be kissed. She'd only shifted back upstairs so news of their separation didn't reach his mother while she wasn't well after all. Maybe he'd imagined her wanting those kisses.

So he'd started burbling on about the soccer team, and her hand had slid from his before they'd reached the front gate—let alone the camellia bush!

But as she lay there, beautiful in the moonlight, he knew they had to patch things up.

He wouldn't think about the baby side of things, instead he would work out the best way for them to be together, slowly and tentatively, a bit like when they had first gone out. Even though what he really wanted was to climb into bed beside her and ravish her right now.

Ravish her?

Where *had* that word come from?

Yet when he considered it, it was apt because

surely the word covered kisses, and touches, and all the joys of foreplay. It covered kissing as much of her skin as he could manage, running his fingers through her hair, nibbling at the little erogenous zones he knew so well—all that and more—far beyond what might be described as sex…

Ravishment?

He padded slowly back to his own room—the room he'd sought refuge in when he'd walked away from her—unable to stay lest they tear each other to pieces even more and end up too wounded to ever recover what they'd had…

Ellie slept well but rose earlier than usual, anxious to see just how much mess remained in the surgery. But when she made her way downstairs after a swift breakfast of tea and toast, she was amazed at what Zeke and Chelsea had accomplished.

True, there was a piece of chipboard where the window should be, but when she opened it, it was barely noticeable and she'd get someone in to repair it during the day.

But the broken glass was gone, all signs of blood mopped up and, in fact, the floors were sparkling clean.

And in the storeroom, where young Logan had obviously rummaged desperately for something to staunch his blood, the first-aid equipment was once more neatly arrayed, the shelves as tidy as Maureen had left them.

Even the black soot from around the safe had been wiped away.

She'd have to thank them both.

'I came in early because I heard you'd had a break-in and wanted to clean up but you've already done it,' Maureen said, looking around in amazement. 'You must have been up at crack of dawn.'

'Not me,' Ellie told her. 'Zeke, the young policeman, and Chelsea did it all last night while Andy and I were at the hospital with our young burglar.'

'I believe it was Logan Grant.' Maureen said with distinct disapproval. 'He really shouldn't be left on his own when his dad's at work, but although Mr Grant's had any number of women in to keep an eye on him, he outwits them all, and sneaks out to do who knows what mischief.'

'Well, we know where he was making mischief yesterday but maybe now he's learned his lesson,' Ellie said, deciding not to reveal the child's reason for the break-in. 'And if we get him to join the soccer team, he'll have less time for mischief.'

Maureen checked that all was well, then settled down to run through the patient list and send it to Ellie's computer, but Ellie was already out of the door.

'It's Chelsea's first day at school,' she said over her shoulder. 'I want to see that she's okay and has everything she needs.'

Upstairs Chelsea was not only ready—in a uniform someone had found for her—but three of the soccer team, including Rangi, were waiting to take her to school.

'Looks like I'll have my own bodyguard,' she joked. But Ellie could see how pleased she was to have someone with her on that nervous first day.

'I've spoken to Mr Grayson, the head teacher, and as soon as you know who your home-room teacher will be, I'll come up and have a talk to him or her as well.'

'I'll be fine,' Chelsea assured her, coming across the kitchen to give Ellie a big hug. Then she stepped back and studied the woman who'd taken her in. 'I think you're more nervous than I am.'

'Probably,' Ellie admitted, wiping her slightly damp hands surreptitiously against her jeans.

But as she stood on the veranda, waving to them as they trooped away, she wondered just how shaken up she'd have been if it was her own child—hers and Andy's—going off to a new school for the first time.

Given how bad she felt, watching Chelsea leave, she had to admit she'd have been a complete mess, and been one of those mothers who stood outside the school gate, sobbing piteously…

Though these days children were introduced to school early. Most would go to kindergarten or preschool first and from there visit whatever school they'd be attending next.

*Good grief!* Was she really leaning on the veranda railing, mooning over a child that would never be—worrying about him or her going to school even…

Ellie headed back down to work, where Maureen tutted because she was all of three minutes late for her first appointment.

The morning passed swiftly, allowing her a little time at the end of her appointments to do some necessary paperwork, then phone Madeleine, who would be on lunch, to check on her knee and general health.

'I've made an appointment with Maureen to come in on Wednesday for the other tests you wanted to run,' Madeleine explained. 'I have a half-day off because there's a Year Nine school excursion to the mine, and the boss doesn't want me walking around too much.'

'Are you the Year Nine home-room teacher?'

Ellie asked, thinking that's where Chelsea would probably fit.

'Yes, I saw Chelsea this morning, and had her for a maths lesson. I think with some extra work over the summer holidays she can skip straight through to Year Eleven in some of her subjects. She's a bright student, very advanced for her age.'

She paused, then added, 'At least that's what I'm hearing from teachers who've already had her in their classes.'

Andy checked on the few hospitalised patients, and the elderly people who lived in the annexe, as the town was too small for a separate retirement village or nursing home.

He had appointments in Outpatients from ten-thirty, but until then he had far too much time on his hands. Too much time to think about Ellie, and whether they *could* get back together again.

Remembering the kisses they'd shared on the veranda, he guessed she was as desperate as he was to sort something out.

Yet he'd shied away from the kiss he'd planned for the camellia bush.

Afraid he might be pushing things too fast?

Afraid—

What *was* he afraid of?

He couldn't answer that thought, although he realised that, somewhere in his head, he'd written off their marriage—had decided it was over.

He'd hurt the woman he loved with his cruel words, could still hurt her if their conversation in the park was anything to go by.

For a long time it seemed that every word he'd spoken had been a brick in the wall he'd—they'd?—built between them, and he had no idea how to break it down.

Had he stopped loving her?

Andy shook his head as much to clear it as by way of an answer.

Because he knew the answer, and had probably known it all along.

A resounding *no*!

Ellie was in his blood, and bones, as much a part of him as a limb…

He loved her with every fibre of his being, yet somehow they'd pummelled each other with words until they'd had to part before the damage to both of them became more severe.

But now?

He banged his hand on the desk, causing the piles of paperwork to flutter into an untidy mess. The bang had been one of frustration at not being able to see a clear path ahead for the two of them, but the fluttering had reminded him of what he *should* be doing, which was some of the never-ending paperwork that came with the job.

A call from Becky, on duty in the ED, saved him from both useless thoughts and paperwork. There had been a traffic accident at a crossing ten kilometres out of town, and the ambulance was already on its way.

Aware they'd send a status report as soon as they'd summed up the situation, Andy went through to the ED to ensure they were prepared for a number of casualties.

He'd barely walked in when the information came clearly from their radio.

Two vehicles, a sedan and a ute, with three injured and a second ambulance on its way. The police were in attendance.

'This is Ted Buckley, the ute driver,' the ambo said, when Andy met the ambulance to help wheel the patient in. 'He was conscious when we reached him, and he's fretting about his dog. Chris has the dog safe in the police car if he asks again.'

Something in the man's voice made Andy ask, 'And *is* the dog safe?'

'It might have a broken leg. I gave him something to keep him comfortable.'

They'd moved Ted into the ED and onto an

examination bed as they'd talked, Andy aware the ambulance would be needed back at the scene.

'Where's Rudi?' Ted demanded, opening his eyes as Andy ran his fingers over the old man's bald head.

'Rudi?' Becky echoed, although Andy guessed he was the dog.

'Me dog!'

'Rudi's fine. Chris is looking after him in the police car.'

'Well, don't let anyone take Rudi,' Ted said. 'Some of the neighbours have been after him for years. Best dog in thc area. One of them gets hold of him I'll never get him back.'

The old man lapsed into silence again.

'We'll X-ray his skull just to be sure, but I can't feel any damage. He'd been wearing his seatbelt because there's just the beginning of bruising diagonally across his chest.'

'*And* driving at about ten kilometres an hour, knowing Ted,' Becky said. 'If anyone's badly injured, the other car must have been speeding.'

And if anyone was badly injured he'd probably need to get Ellie back in again.

An image of her as she'd lain in bed the previous night flashed into Andy's head, and remembering the thoughts he'd had then spread warmth through his body. He had to win Ellie back and somehow make their marriage work—no, more than that, make them one again.

They'd have to talk, but this time openly, honestly and carefully so as not to make things worse. If he could explain about the baby, how he felt…

Andy had already spoken to a counselling service and was hoping to find someone he could speak to regularly. He had to sort himself out before he could really sort out his marriage…

The other accident victims arrived, thankfully having sustained little injury.

The driver had a high ankle injury, probably to the syndesmosis tendon, a tear that would require him walking around in a moon boot for a month but not needing plaster, while the passenger beside him had escaped with nothing more than cuts and bruises. Andy decided to keep them both in hospital under observation in case there was anything more serious.

But there was another victim that had everyone excited, the female nurses particularly. A fine baby girl, maybe five or six months old, kept safe by her state-of-the-art car seat, was looking around the ED with huge blue eyes, apparently up for any adventure that came her way.

'Well, she's the last thing you'd expect those

two larrikins to be travelling with,' Becky said. 'I doubt she belongs to either of them.'

'The car seat is top of the range, and her clothing looks expensive, too. Do any of you know the two lads?'

There were head shakes all round, though Becky, who'd lifted the baby from her car seat and was giving her a cuddle, said, 'I agree about the young men's scruffy clothes.'

They all stared at the baby girl, who smiled obligingly at them all, reaching out to grasp some tinsel that hung from the reception desk and drag it towards her mouth before Becky removed it firmly from her grasp.

'She's gorgeous, isn't she?' Andy said, aware that the small mortal was already winning a way into hearts normally hardened by the stresses and sights of the ED.

'She needs changing. There are boxes of nappies in the storeroom at the back of the building,' Becky said, and one of the aides hurried off to find them.

But Andy was transfixed by the child.

*She's been in an accident, you should be examining her*, a voice in his head was insisting, and although he knew the voice was right, he just knew that she was fine.

Although as Becky began to change her nappy, he finally stepped forward.

'We'd better take a look at her,' he said, and helped Becky peel off the jumpsuit she was wearing.

But the little body was unmarked, no sign of the accident at all.

But as Becky started to dress her again, something struck Andy.

'I know baby skin needs protection but isn't that jumpsuit too hot for her to be wearing on a summer's day? It's more like something she might wear on a cool night.'

Becky stared at their young charge, lying on the now discarded piece of clothing.

'You're right,' she said. 'It *was* cool last night, even out here. Maybe the mother's ill and those lads are taking her to stay with relatives?'

She sounded so doubtful Andy knew she didn't believe that particular scenario for one instant.

'See if you can find a light top for her—even a singlet—then turn on the local radio, see if there's a report about a missing baby,' Andy suggested. 'I'll go and speak to the lads.'

But he had the same reaction from both of them.

'What baby? We don't know anything about a baby! It must have been the old fellow's.'

Realising it was pointless pushing them further, he phoned Chris, who confirmed the baby had come out of the lads' car and it had puzzled him as well.

'They're denying she was in their car, let alone had anything to do with them,' Andy told him, and heard Chris sigh.

'Well, someone called Lydia Francks is the registered owner of the car, but we can't contact her at the address she gave for her licence. I'll send someone up to question the lads, not that they'd get far out of town without a vehicle. Don't let them go until someone gets there.'

Andy smiled.

'I doubt they'll want to go,' he said. 'We stripped off their clothes to examine them properly and they're both wearing very fetching hospital nightgowns.'

He heard Chris's answering laugh.

'I do hope they're the ones that are open all down the back.'

But as Andy made his way back to the two newest admissions to check their clothing had been removed from their rooms, his mind was on the baby.

Someone *had* to be missing her.

And she must have been in a car somewhere, given that she was still in her car seat...

Surely she couldn't have been left in a car park? At this time of the year, even a short time in a locked car could kill a young child, the summer heat baking the interior to over fifty degrees centigrade.

She was happy so she was presumably not hungry. Had they fed her something or had she been fed just before they had taken her?

He checked the young men's clothes had been bagged and passed to the ward secretary, not back to the owners. And much as he'd have liked to question the two himself, he knew that Chris or one of his men would have far more expertise in that area than he had, even though questions were a huge part of his job.

He had appointments in Outpatients, yet was drawn back to the ED, where Becky was now cuddling the baby as she fed her a bottle.

'Good thing we keep baby formula in stock,' she said, as the baby broke off her noisy guzzling to bestow a milky smile on Andy.

It made his heart hurt and he hurried away.

*No more. Never again.*

The words were like a mantra as he strode through the hospital on his way to the people waiting for him.

# CHAPTER SEVEN

ZEKE BROUGHT THE dog to Ellie's surgery during what would normally be her lunch hour.

'They're busy at the hospital with the three accident victims and the baby, so I thought you might be able to take a look at Rudi. Ted just adores this dog, and he'd hate anything to happen to him.'

He was carrying the mildly sedated dog gently in his arms, and while Maureen scolded about hygiene and being a doctor's surgery, not a vet's, Ellie ran her fingers over the dog. With no vet in town, she'd known she might come up against injured pets, but this dog was her first. She'd grown up with dogs, so had a fair knowledge of broken limbs and battered heads, but Rudi, as far as she could see and feel, was fine.

Until she pressed his left rear foot, and he snatched it away with a yelp. Lifting it more gently this time, she examined the pad for a tear or a foreign object lodged in it, but could find no damage. Was it the joint?

Tentatively, she moved the foot, and this time Rudi had recovered enough to growl at her.

'I think I'll just bind it reasonably tightly and we'll see if he can put weight on it. Can you hold him while I do it?'

She was pleased when Zeke nodded, because she really didn't fancy putting Rudi on her examination couch, no matter how many sheets of paper she'd spread beneath him.

'Tell me about the baby,' she said to Zeke, as she worked to stabilise the ankle.

Zeke shrugged his shoulders.

'She was in the back of the sedan that ran into Ted. Two young lads—the driver and a passenger—both denying any knowledge of a baby in a very smart safety seat in their vehicle. They're lying, of course. From the baby stuff we found in the car—bottles and formula—at least one of them had enough gumption to realise she'd need to be fed.'

'A car theft and they didn't realise the baby was there until it was too late?' Ellie guessed. 'But someone must be missing her.'

Ellie led the way outside so they could try Rudi on his legs.

'You'd think so,' Zeke told her, as he gently

put Rudi on the ground, keeping a firm hold on his collar in case he took off.

Rudi moved cautiously, but within minutes was using all four feet.

'Now, what do we do with him?' Zeke asked.

'Well, we don't have a proper fence here so maybe he could go in one of your nice cells, just until his master is sorted at the hospital.'

Zeke smiled at her, and bent to gather the dog into his arms again, carrying him over to the police car and strapping him into the back seat.

'Thanks!' he said, then seemed to hover by the car, eventually coming out with what was bothering him.

'Does Andy want any older players on his soccer team, or perhaps someone to help with things?'

Ellie beamed at him.

'I'm sure he'd be delighted to have you. As far as I can see, it's a kind of "the more the merrier" situation.'

Ellie stood there as he drove away. Was his interest in soccer or Chelsea?

Not that it mattered, but she'd keep an eye on things.

She was turning to go into the house when a council truck pulled up across the street, men and ladders tumbling out of it.

'It can't be that close to Christmas!' she

wailed as she watched the men begin their decorating.

But looking further down the street, she saw that Christmas decorations were already up, all the way to town—and hadn't she seen some at the hospital?

Christmas had sneaked up on her without her realising it. One year ago, they had spent the day with her family, a boisterous reunion of siblings, aunts, uncles and her one remaining grandparent.

She had been due to start IVF in the New Year, and was imagining another Christmas—the next one—perhaps with them as a family of three…

She had to stop thinking about it, and the memories that caused so much pain. Yet weren't the memories what kept Andy and her together? Weren't they the reason she knew she wanted to put things right between them again?

Logan had thought money might bring his mother home for Christmas, but wasn't it love that cemented a marriage and kept it strong?

And she knew she still loved Andy and was almost certain he loved her, so how could they bridge the gap between them?

At least they were getting closer, holding hands, kissing even…

And as memories of that last kiss they'd

shared sent shivers down her spine she knew that, come what may, they *had* to heal the rift.

She knew she'd started the argument that had led to the final straw for Andy with the suggestion of one last go at IVF, but why had it escalated?

Had she been too stubborn about it?

Was she still aching to hold her own child in her arms?

Ellie tried to push the thought away but a spark of it must have remained that she finally walked up the stairs and into the house, rubbing at the frown line she knew was on her forehead.

But if she wanted Andy—and she knew now just how much she *did* want him—then she had to accept that it would never be.

She had to kill that spark of hope that still nestled deep inside her, and get on with her life.

She'd reached the veranda before she realised she was supposed to be at work, so back down the stairs she went, dead-heating at the door with Andy, who was holding a beautiful baby in his arms.

Was this the baby Zeke had mentioned?

'I've admitted two cases of measles to the hospital this morning so she can't stay there,' Andy was saying as he handed her the baby. 'Do you think that you and Maureen could keep an eye on her? Chris's wife went down to

Croxton for last-minute Christmas shopping and there's really no one else even semi-official. I'll just get her car seat.'

The baby girl was sound asleep, as angelic as only sleeping children could be.

'But —' Ellie began, and realised she was speaking to space as Andy had dropped the car seat and a bag containing nappies, bottles, and formula on the floor and was already gone.

'*Can* we cope?' she said to Maureen, the weight and warmth of the infant feeling so right, Ellie knew that killing that spark of hope she'd been thinking about only minutes earlier might prove impossible.

'While she sleeps, I suppose we can,' Maureen replied a trifle tautly.

'Well, Chelsea will be home from school before long, so I guess we can manage until then.'

Andy drove back to the hospital in the police car he'd borrowed to deliver the baby. His chest felt tight and his stomach knotted. The sight of Ellie with the baby in her arms had awoken all the stuff he'd been desperately trying to put behind him.

She'd looked so right, and natural.

He tamped down the panic that thought brought with it, and the pain that he'd thought he'd conquered. He closed his eyes and tried to see ahead to their future, his and Ellie's, when they were back together again.

He remembered the kisses they'd shared. The passion they'd known was still there, he knew that much, he just had to—

*What?*

Tell her how he'd felt? How much it had hurt? Still hurt?

Did he blame her for not knowing—not seeing it for herself?

Hardly, when she'd been so grief-stricken and racked with blame that hadn't been hers at all…

But now things were easing between them, maybe they could talk about that time without the emotion that had ripped them apart.

If only they could talk, and touch, and ease their way back into the love he knew was still there between them…

Chris's voice came through the vehicle's radio. There was still no lost baby alert, and no idea as to who she could be.

But the baby wasn't Andy's problem. Chris could deal with that. His focus, apart from work, had to be on Ellie, and their future.

He'd just pulled into the hospital car park when his phone rang. It was Ellie.

Chris brought the news that the baby had been identified. Her nanny had been found and had admitted she'd put the baby in the car to drive her around for a while to get her to sleep, then stopped at a corner store for cigarettes, leaving not only the baby but the keys in the car.

The temptation had been too great for the two lads. They'd got a lift down to the coast with a friend, and right in front of them was a car, keys inside, just waiting for them.

Although they'd gone a fair distance before they'd realised they'd had a passenger, and then only when she'd cried.

One of them now admitted having younger siblings and knew enough to assume the baby was hungry so they'd stopped in Croxton, gone to a chemist and bought a bottle and some baby formula, fed the baby and, for lack of any other idea, driven on.

Undaunted by this lack of a plan, they'd told themselves they were doing the baby a favour as she shouldn't have been left in the car in the first place—everyone knew that children could die in hot cars…

From that point on their stories varied. They were taking the baby to the nearest police station when they had the accident, or were turning to go back and leave the car where they'd found it. Either way, the baby remained safe.

'But what happened to the nanny?' Ellie demanded, as Chris was explaining all of this to her, Andy and Chelsea, who was now back from school and delighted by the baby.

'Well, she was too frightened to admit that she'd lost her charge so she ran off to a friend's house. It was the friend who convinced her to contact the police and the parents.'

'She'd have panicked, that's only natural,' Ellie said. 'But at least she did the right thing in the end.'

'Anyway, the parents are on their way. They should be here in a couple of hours,' Chris told them. 'Are you okay to keep her here?'

Andy smiled at him.

'I think you'd be hard pushed to get her away,' he said, nodding to where Chelsea now rocked the baby in her arms.

But when Chris left to get back to work, Andy suggested they put the baby into her car seat to sleep.

'Babies can get very heavy when you're holding them for a long time,' he added, smiling at Chelsea, who nodded but let go reluctantly, watching to see Andy carefully secure the little one in her seat, talking quietly to her as he did it, although she was asleep.

And with the job finished, he stayed there, squatting in front of her and reaching out to run a finger down her cheek, and touch her tiny hand.

'I've got homework,' Chelsea announced, when they were all happy that the baby had slept through the move.

'And I could do with a cup of coffee,' Andy said, straightening up and walking swiftly away from the distraction. 'I have to go back to the hospital, but it's been such a weird day I feel a need a break to catch up with myself.'

'Sit down and I'll get it,' Ellie told him, and as she pottered around the kitchen, turning the machine on, getting out mugs, she felt more at ease with Andy than she had for months.

'So, what was *your* impression of Chelsea and the baby?' Andy asked, the question so unexpected she needed a moment to process it.

'Well,' she began cautiously, 'it could just be normal teenage girl reaction to a baby. With all the hormonal stuff going on inside them, I think that's only natural.'

'You don't sound too sure,' Andy said, smiling at her teasingly, because he knew she was usually definite in her opinions.

'I'm not,' she admitted, 'and neither, I imagine, is Chelsea. It's probably created all kinds of emotions inside her, and raised so many doubts and issues in me, so I hope her homework is very difficult, and absolutely has to be done for tomorrow.'

She sighed.

'We might talk about it over dinner,' she suggested, and Andy nodded, finished his coffee, and stood up.

'Lacking any very difficult homework, I'd better get back to work.'

And just like that he left, Ellie staring after him, puzzling over his words.

Could he really be saying he'd felt something in his heart as he'd held the baby, secured her safely in her seat and knelt in front of her for those extra minutes…?

A longing?

Or just sadness?

Ellie knew she was frowning.

Ellie went down to the surgery to check on the next day's patients and finish off some paperwork. She really had to get Chelsea in for an ultrasound sometime soon, and suspected she was putting it off as it was going to make the baby more real to both of them.

And for all she told herself that Chelsea was just a patient like any other, she couldn't help but feel connected to the new life growing inside their guest.

Was she jealous?

She didn't think so.

Just uneasy, somehow…

'Forget it!' Ellie muttered to herself, checking the appointments book on the computer and putting Chelsea down for a scan after school the following Monday. 'Think about Andy instead!'

And this second order made her smile, although there was definitely a little flutter in the region of her heart.

She was saved further speculation by the sounds of arrivals, as at least two vehicles pulled up outside.

She slipped out of the surgery, locking the door behind her, in time to hear a man saying in a determined voice, 'And just where are these so-called lads? I'll need their details. I'm going to sue them, you know. Get them for the pain and torment they've caused Melissa and I.'

'Melissa and me,' Ellie corrected beneath her breath, already disliking this pompous man who, as far as she was concerned, definitely didn't deserve such a beautiful daughter.

'The law will take care of the lads,' Chris said firmly. 'It's the baby you'll both be wanting to see.'

'She's just upstairs,' Ellie said. 'I was going to give her a quick sponge over before you came. It's been a hot, dusty day.'

Andy arrived from the hospital at that stage, full of his usual good cheer.

'I'll do that,' he said. 'Now, come on up, you'll be anxious to see her.'

The newcomers followed, and even when they arrived in the living room and saw their daughter safe and sound—in her car seat—the only reaction from the mother was, 'Why is she wearing that old singlet?' although she did go and kneel by the chair and kiss the forehead of her sleeping child.

'It was all we had at the hospital that was cool,' Andy said.

'Did you bring clothes for her?' Ellie asked.

Both shook their heads.

She paused, and Andy, only half-aware of what she might be about to say, held his breath.

'I've got some clothes you can have for her. In fact, if Zeke wouldn't mind going back to the hospital for more formula, you could bath her and change her here, then feed her and she should sleep on the trip back.'

'Leave the bath to me,' Andy said, aware that the offer of clothes must have caused Ellie enough pain and wanting to distract any attention from her.

'Well, I suppose as a doctor you can do this kind of thing,' the father said, and Andy had to close his lips on the retort that most men could do it.

'Actually, I'm happy to do it,' he growled. 'Babies are great.'

Zeke had disappeared on his errand and Ellie

had also left the room, but he knew where she'd be, and knew what clothes she'd find for the baby.

He followed her into the small room off the side of the room Ellie used. Thank heavens they had been too busy settling in to decorate it in preparation for *their* baby. It was bad enough that it still had a small chest of drawers, filled with baby clothes and gifts from friends and relations when they'd left the city…

Ellie had the second drawer open and was running her fingertips over the contents.

'It's a good thing we've got intelligent friends so we were given clothes in every size from preemie to two years old.'

He could hear the battle she was having to keep her anguish out of her voice.

Andy came fully into the small room and wrapped his arms around her, holding her tightly, feeling the tension drain from her body as tears she'd tried to hold back slid down her cheeks.

'It will be all right,' he whispered against her hair. 'We'll work things out. You know I love you—I always have and always will—the rest's just been a distraction.'

She looked up into his eyes, her own pinkened by her tears.

'You really believe that?'

He tightened his grip on her, and kissed her lips, the softness of them startling his nerves and tightening his body.

'You know I do,' he said against them, and felt her mouth open, her tongue touch his, electrifying every cell in his body.

'We should get going,' she whispered to him, when it seemed they'd stood like that for an age.

'We probably should,' he said, but he continued to hold her, just a little longer, while all the memories of the passion they'd shared welled up in their bodies until the effort of breaking apart was one of extreme willpower.

'Later!' he murmured in her ear, then he wiped the tears from her cheeks and took the tiny garments from her as she lifted them carefully from the drawer.

'I'll get some warm water to sponge her down,' she said, her voice shaky but determined. 'And a couple of towels.

Glad to have something to do, Ellie hurried to get what Andy would need, depositing the towels and water on the coffee table, spreading one towel so Andy could put the baby on it.

Aware that her eyes would be red and tears not far away, she then retreated, going into the kitchen and staring unseeingly into the fridge because she was fairly sure she should be doing something about dinner.

But the feel of Andy's arms around her, the hardness of his body as he'd held her close, stayed with her, stirring her senses and tightening her body.

She was still staring at the meagre contents of the fridge when Chelsea breezed into the kitchen.

'Is it okay if Zeke takes me to the Thai place for dinner? A few of the soccer team are going. Someone's birthday, I think.'

'As long as you're home by ten,' Ellie said, glad to be distracted from the tumult of her body. 'It's a school night, remember.'

'Yes, Mum,' Chelsea teased, and she slipped away, pausing as she passed the living room to call out, 'Goodbye, baby!'

Ellie closed the fridge and sat down at the kitchen table, resting her elbows on it, with her head in her hands. She heard the sound of movement and knew the unwanted guests were departing, but she felt no obligation to speak to them again, so she was still sitting there when Andy returned to announce that everyone was gone.

He slumped into a chair opposite her.

'I can't believe that was so hard,' he said, staring up at the ceiling.

'The baby?'

He nodded, then turned to her, reaching out to take her hand.

'And I can only imagine what you felt, taking that little outfit out of the drawer and handing it over. Your baby's clothes—*our* baby's clothes. Oh, Ellie, darling, it's been one shit of a year, hasn't it?'

He stood up now, and walked around the table to pull her to her feet, take her in his arms, hold her tightly.

'I thought my heart would break back then.'

The words startled Ellie so much she couldn't speak, only hold him as close as he was holding her.

'I didn't know,' she whispered. 'I didn't know how you felt. I was too wrapped up in my own misery to even think about the man I loved.'

'Well, at least you knew you still loved him—me,' he whispered, 'at times I even wondered about that.'

'Oh, Andy, what a mess we've made of things—I've made of things. I was so exhausted, so lost, but I should have made time for you.'

'No, you were right the first time—*we* made the mess—and it's understandable when you think about how traumatic it was for us at the time.'

She raised her head and looked at him, at the

face she knew so well, the dark eyes smiling quizzically at her, the love he felt for her there, shining in them.

'Take me to bed, Andy?' she said quietly, and he turned with his arm around her shoulder and slowly and silently they walked through to the bedroom.

By which time Ellie was shaking so badly she wasn't sure she'd manage to take off her clothes, but Andy, who seemed to have similar tremors, somehow managed to get them both naked. In a matter of moments they stood, running their hands over each other's bodies, learning them again through touch, then taste as their lips met, desperately seeking each other, teeth clashing, tongues twining, lips moving over skin now—

'Bed?'

Andy breathed the word into her ear, and within minutes their hunger for each other had them joined in a frantic coupling, murmurs of love and pleasure providing a soundtrack to their passion.

They lay spent, their bodies still entwined, remembering the feel of skin on skin, the cries of their release; remembering how things used to be…

And could be again?

Ellie smiled, knowing it not only could but would.

'Hungry?' Andy asked, and when she nodded sleepily against him, he eased away and she heard him rattling around in the kitchen. She was half-asleep when he returned, bearing a tray with two small but perfect omelettes on it, cutlery for two, two wine glasses, and a bottle tucked under his arm.

It was if the last few months had never been—as if it was only yesterday Andy had cooked an omelette for her, and brought it to her in bed.

They talked of the weird day they'd had, of Ted Buckley, and Rudi the dog, about everything but the baby and the clothes she had worn as she'd left the house.

Then sleep overtook them both, but it was deep and dreamless, their bodies still curled together, once again...

But as the dawn chorus of the magpies and butcher birds woke them, to a pink sky announcing the coming dawn, they turned to each other, and slowly, languorously made love again.

Taking their time to learn each other again, prolonging the passion that built between them until it consumed them in a fiery blaze of lust and left them sated, exhausted on the sweat-drenched sheets, with no words for this reunion—this miracle of love returned...

# CHAPTER EIGHT

COULD IT REALLY have been so simple? Ellie wondered a week later. Could she and Andy have slipped back into their old passionate relationship so easily?

Even thinking about what happened in bed excited her, sending warmth flooding through her body and desire tautening her nerves.

At work, she had to concentrate to put thoughts of Andy right away, but not as far away as they had been…

She took the tests Madeleine would need for the specialist in Sydney, arranging for her to get copies of the results. She scanned Chelsea's bump but didn't reveal the sex of the baby, something Chelsea had decided she didn't want to know.

Work was less busy as people prepared for Christmas. The stores along the main road were bright with lights, each trying to outdo each other with their Christmas decorations.

But the phone call from the local newspaper was totally unexpected.

Would she please judge the decorated houses? They had prizes for the best house and the best street, where neighbours got together to light up the skies with Christmas cheer.

'I'm not sure I'd be up to that,' she told the young man who'd phoned her.

'It's simple,' he said. 'The other Mrs Dr Fraser always did it. The judging is tomorrow night. I can pick you up at seven if that's okay?'

Tomorrow night?

Andy came home as she was frowning over this latest assignment.

'I've got to judge the best decorated house,' she told him, and he laughed.

'It's easy, Mum always did it. She reckoned the winner always stood out.'

'Oh, yeah? Well, I think I'd better have a practice run tonight. Will you come with me?'

'If you really think it's necessary.'

Andy was hardly enthusiastic, although when they finally set out, Chelsea having joined them, it turned into a riotous affair, with all of them choosing different houses, then changing their minds about it when they saw the next one.

The decorations were unbelievable. Santa rode his light-festooned sleigh across one rooftop, and was clambering down a chimney on another. In some gardens he'd be surrounded by his elves, all animated so they seemed to be making toys, while others were more a light and sound show with Christmas carols playing against lights that changed and seemed to dance with the music.

Even the mine was decorated. Although some kilometres out of town, the tall structure that operated the lift was ablaze with coloured lights.

'You're both hopeless and no help at all,' Ellie told them, when they'd completed the circuit of decorated houses for the second time.

But the following night she was glad she'd checked them out, because it became easier to see who'd put the most work into the colourful spectacles, and she settled on the house with Santa's sleigh on the roof. The sheer effort of getting it and a rotund Santa up there deserved a reward.

But seeing how much effort people put into their decorations made Ellie realise she and Andy had done nothing to decorate their own house. So finally she found the courage to investigate the shed where she knew Andy's parents had left their Christmas decorations, claiming there were far too many for the small apartment they'd moved to at the coast.

Maureen had already decorated the surgery

with tinsel and baubles and a small tree, which had all been stored away to be used year after year.

So it was left to Ellie and Chelsea—and Logan, who'd turned up to do some gardening—to decorate the house. Andy was still too involved in shifting people about in his soccer team, or teams as it was now, to be much help. They began on the veranda, stringing lights along the railing and hanging twinkling stars from the posts that supported the roof.

And the air in the house was lighter somehow, warm with love and laughter, the excitement of Christmas an added bonus.

'Chelsea and I are going down to Croxton this afternoon,' Ellie announced at breakfast, on the second last day of the school term. 'It's late-night shopping and she needs some clothes.'

Andy looked across the table at her and smiled.

'And you don't? How long since you've been to that boutique you love down there? Buy yourself something special for Christmas—something from me.'

Far too much in love to be offended by this male attitude to gift-giving, Ellie simply smiled. She'd already done most of her Christmas shopping online, and had even found the perfect gift for Andy—an elaborate watch that could time the practice drills he did with his team and about a hundred other things she didn't understand but knew he would.

Christmas fever was spreading through the town. People were already wearing T-shirts with reindeer heads or snowmen on them, and white pom-pommed Santa hats as they shopped in forty-degree Celsius heat.

And this Saturday would be the town's Christmas parade, which acted as a celebration of the end of the school year as well as being less than a week to go before the big day. The soccer team would be marching in it, most of them now in uniform, although some of the younger newcomers, like Logan and his mates, might have to make do with yellow T-shirts.

Chelsea had made a bright yellow flag and appointed herself to carry it at the head of their group. The 'Maytown Soccer Club' emblazoned across it would be held proud for all to see.

When they were in town Ellie did visit the boutique in Croxton, finding there a lovely, slinky, satin nightdress in a soft oyster colour that felt so sexy on that she blushed in the changing room.

But as she slipped into it that night, she wondered if she should have kept it for Christmas night, and made *it* the gift from Andy.

But the glow of physical love and satisfaction

had her in its thrall. Everything was going so well—they were Andy and Ellie again, at one with each other, their love as strong as ever.

Maybe even stronger?

So she wanted to feel the tempting garment on her—for him to see it on her—to have him take it off…

'Is this my Christmas present to you?' he asked, smiling as she twirled in front of him later that night, the soft material clinging to every curve of her figure.

'No,' she whispered, 'it's mine to you.'

She put her arms around him, kissed his lips, then said, 'Stand still.'

And slowly, teasingly, she removed his clothes, pressing kisses against skin as it was bared, trailing her fingers over the body she knew so well.

They made love slowly, hands and lips exploring, until a single touch from Andy's finger sent Ellie spiralling into space, her body still tingling as Andy entered her, and teased her into another climax, matching it to his own.

And afterwards, lying on their sides, facing each other, Ellie traced his profile with her finger, traced his lips, his ears, the little whorl in his hair above his left eyebrow…

This was how life was meant to be—hers and Andy's. Surely now they could go on as they had begun, not only in love but in tune with each other. They could share their work and their interests—well, she'd go to *some* of the soccer games—but working together they could offer so much to the community, while their own lives would be enriched by their participation in it.

And just perhaps...

She was so filled with happiness, so in love with this man, that it seemed only natural to speak about a thought that had occurred to her earlier today.

'Do you know?' she began in a drowsy, satisfied voice. 'I hadn't realised until today but this week has probably been a very fertile time for me. Though I can't be sure—you know how irregular I am. Do you think, after all these years and the IVF and everything, we could be lucky enough for it to happen just like that?'

But Andy was out of bed before she'd finished her question, grabbing at his shorts, hauling them on, his face ablaze with anger.

'You seduced me! You tricked me! Take me to bed, Andy, you said, when all along you knew how I felt about another baby— all along you knew I couldn't go through that again.'

He snatched his pillow from the bed and marched away, through the en suite bathroom and back to the other bedroom—the bliss and happiness of the last week dissolving in front of her, his harsh words of blame cutting her heart into pieces…

She didn't cry—couldn't. Perhaps she'd already used up her life's allotment of tears.

Or perhaps the shock and pain was too deep for tears…

She closed her eyes and tried to work out why he had reacted as he had. Yes, he'd said no to more IVF but surely…?

What did he feel about it all that she should know?

Andy had been upset, yes, they both had…

But had she crawled into herself with her misery, wrapping it around her like a cocoon? Had she not shared it, not talked enough with Andy about how he might have been feeling?

Back then Ellie had assumed his 'no more IVF' had meant he just didn't want to go through the whole process again, and, in truth, neither had she. Not really. The drugs had made her feel ill at times, and at other moments the process had seemed so clinical she'd wondered if she could care for a baby conceived this way as much as one she'd carried from day one in her womb.

And while their love-making had left her languid, that feeling had turned to one of devastation.

How could she not have known Andy's feelings about another baby? How could she have simply assumed he was over the IVF process and it was her suggestion of that which had shattered their happiness?

What *did* Andy feel?

And worst of all, how did she not know?

Morning brought no answers. Andy had already gone by the time she reached the kitchen. In fact, Chelsea was ready to leave as well, a watermelon for the final-day festivities tucked under one arm.

'Have fun!' Ellie said to Chelsea, and hoped the words hadn't sounded as hollow as they felt.

But as she worked through the day she knew she couldn't go back to the way things had been recently. She wanted a real marriage or none at all.

She had to talk to Andy.

But Andy was conspicuous by his absence. He was off organising something with the soccer team, Chelsea told her as they ate their dinner.

'There are no games tomorrow because of the parade, but he wanted to sort out how they'd march so they looked professional rather than a rabble.'

'And you're not there?' Ellie asked.

Chelsea smiled at her.

'You know I'm the flag bearer. I know where I've got to go.'

'*And* there are more uniforms,' Chelsea continued. 'The butcher has decided to sponsor us and he donated them—well, him and his customers—he's got a box on his counter collecting money for us.'

'Good for him,' Ellie said, and felt the warmth she kept finding in this small community, the sense of everyone pitching in to help, no matter what.

*Could* she move away?

She'd talk to Andy, first time she had a chance, and convince him she'd been feeling so happy the words had just come out. She'd apologise for upsetting him and try to get him to talk about whatever he was feeling…

But he was gone again the next morning.

'He's organising off-duty hospital staff to be posted along the parade route,' Chelsea informed her. 'In case anyone faints.'

'Humph!'

Ellie hadn't realised she'd actually let her disbelief out until Chelsea raised her eyebrows at her.

'You'll see him at the parade,' Chelsea reminded her, but a fat lot of good that would do.

She could hardly yell an apology at him as he marched past with his soccer team.

Chelsea headed off, and Ellie cleaned up the breakfast things, swept the kitchen, and had a cool shower. It was already hot, and unless she could find some shady spot on the parade route, she was going to get even hotter.

In shorts and a tank top, sandals on her feet, she slapped a wide-brimmed hat on her head and set off, all the anticipation she'd felt earlier for this annual event draining from her.

Ellie wouldn't come, Andy decided as he lined his players up behind the rugby boys and girls. She'd been so excited and he'd virtually slapped her down, killed that happiness he'd seen in her eyes. Damn it all, how could he not explain, not tell her how he'd felt? But remembered pain had torn through his body, piercing his heart and opening up old wounds and the deep black hole and before he'd known it, the words had come tumbling out.

He tried to concentrate on the parade—on what he was supposed to be doing—but in his head he could see the colour leaving Ellie's face, the light dying in her eyes, as he'd rounded on her…

He tried to shut out the memories and think about the parade. Cubs and Scouts, Guides and

Brownies led the way, then the rugby lot, his soccer team, a band from the school, and a series of floats and special attractions, including stiltwalkers and dancing girls in parade order all the way down the main street and into the park.

He walked with his team, but his mind wasn't on it, his eyes sweeping the crowd that lined the street.

Ellie still might come…

And even if she didn't, did that mean anything?

She could have had an emergency…

*Or* he might have ruined things between them for ever.

His gut twisted.

He could hear the yells of delight from the crowd so the fire engine, resplendent in tinsel and balloons, with Father Christmas sitting on his throne on the tank at the back, must have come into view. The yells of delight were probably the fact that he was throwing wrapped sweets into the crowd.

He could hear the cries of the children, and see the smiling faces. It was Christmas, a time of joy, and here he was wondering if he'd ever feel such an emotion again.

Although his heart *did* do its customary flip when he saw Ellie—picked her out fifty metres away—squashed in beside a couple of women he recognised as soccer mums. At least she'd come…

He'd escaped the house early this morning, on the pretext of having to check in at the hospital before heading over to the marshalling ground for the parade.

Deep down he knew he should have stayed and talked and tried to explain to her just how much the loss of their unborn child had hurt him. His counsellor had told him that was the place to start. But how to explain something he couldn't explain even to himself. It was a black hole in his head, with its own black cloud that hovered above him when he remembered that time.

He'd turned his attention back to the team when he saw two figures fly out of the crowd, a man and a woman, the woman middle-aged, the man younger.

He was at the back of the group to hurry along the stragglers so he couldn't see their faces but as they'd now reached Chelsea and had practically strangled her with hugs, he wondered if it could be her family—her mother, who had just been found—and her brother, Harry.

To their credit, his squad barely faltered in their steps, and somehow Chelsea had sorted out the newcomers, who were now marching with her, one each side, beaming at the crowd and giving little waves.

He caught sight of Ellie in the crowd again, waving with all the onlookers.

Was it possible that she'd pulled this latest stunt on him because she really hadn't known what he'd been through when their unborn baby had died?

Andy thought back to that terrible time, to their shock and pain—shared at first, then as the reality had sunk in, Ellie, though exhausted by her grief, had gone back to work, determined not to let her patients and the town down.

Work had become her escape from thinking, as it had for him much earlier.

And, if Andy was honest, how could Ellie have known when he'd found it impossible to talk about—to even think about most of the time…

He couldn't go back to living as they had been, before they'd ended up in the same bed again. They had to talk—just talk this time—without the pain and hurt and harshness that had followed their loss…

Ellie searched for Andy at the showground, where the parade had ended. A fair had been set up for the children, hot dog stalls, and baked potatoes with a dozen different fillings.

A search of the beer tent, which was only slightly more crowded than the local women's group tent supplying tea, with scones and jam and cream, failed to produce her husband, so Ellie settled for the latter, gratefully accepting the tepid-looking tea as she'd finished the water from the bottle she carried by the time the parade had only been halfway through.

She still wanted to find Andy, to talk to him, but now she'd had her tea and settled down, she realised that somewhere a little less public than these festivities would be more appropriate.

Chelsea had found him first, so when Ellie saw them under a big eucalypt, talking to a young man and a vaguely familiar-looking woman, she wondered if she should interfere.

But Chelsea beckoned her over, her face bright with happiness.

'You'll never guess who came,' she said, almost glowing with pride. 'My mum and Harry. Here they are.'

Ellie looked at them, remembering now how pretty Chelsea's mother was, although it had been years since she'd seen her. And Harry was now a handsome young man.

Jill was effusive in her thanks for them looking after Chelsea, trying to explain what had led her to taking off and leaving her two children behind.

'It was stupid,' she said. 'I've known since before I married Ken that he'd always be off somewhere, worrying about the planet, but this last time, when he left, I felt let down, useless and unnecessary to requirements. The kids were practically grown up and before long they'd be gone, and I began to worry about who I really was if I wasn't a mother or a wife—which is all I'd been for a long time.'

Ellie nodded. Her mother had been much the same when she, Ellie, had left home—cast adrift somehow, until she'd decided to go back to school.

'I do understand,' she said to Jill. 'But at least you're here now, and Chelsea knows you'll be with her through the months ahead.'

'Me, too,' said Harry as Jill hugged her daughter, apologising for all that had happened and promising they'd work things out together.

But Jill was still trying to explain.

'I should never have left! I love my family, I really do, and what made me think I needed more than that—needed something special—I don't know.'

'Probably Dad spending half his life away from us,' Harry said, putting his arms around his mother and giving her a hug.

'Yes, but you both know that when we are together, we more than make up for it.'

Ellie thought of the nights she'd shared with Andy recently and couldn't have agreed more.

Until she'd accidentally spoiled it.

Or had she?

Ellie looked at Andy and read the anguish in his eyes. She touched his arms just lightly, and was pleased when he didn't pull away but actually smiled at her.

'They've driven up from Sydney, so I've asked them to stay, at least for one night, before they drive back,' he said.

And Ellie echoed the invitation, insisting they come to the house now to have a shower and cool off from the heat.

'I'll show them the way,' Chelsea said, linking her arms through theirs, so she had family on both sides.

'I've got to stay a while,' Andy said. 'I don't like leaving the younger ones without a responsible adult with them.'

'I don't blame you for that,' Ellie said as she spied Logan climbing into one of the cars on the octopus ride. 'But, Andy, I do want to say something.'

He met her eyes, but his were cautious. There was none of the warmth and love she'd read in them recently.

'I didn't take you to bed deliberately. I had no idea how you felt about the baby. I just needed you so badly that night, needed your love and your loving. It was only later that I realised, and mentioned it because I thought you'd be happy.'

He stared at her for a moment, then shook his head.

'You have no idea how it made me feel, losing our baby. How much it hurt, the things it killed inside me,' he said, and turned away.

Ellie watched him go.

Was that it?

Was it over?

Did the week they'd just shared mean nothing to him?

The years they'd shared less than nothing…?

*That was not happening*, she decided. And now at least she had a clue. She'd had no idea how he'd felt—that's what he'd said.

Looking back, she'd known he'd been as upset about losing the baby as she had been, and they'd grieved together.

But had it been more than that to Andy?

Some deeper, more visceral pain that had made him adamant he couldn't go through it again.

And instead of talking properly, instead of listening to him, learning how he felt, she'd wrapped her own unhappiness around her like a shroud, ignoring him…

And later, she remembered only the cruel

words he'd thrown at her and how she'd hit back at him, until they'd had to stop before they'd destroyed each other.

But now?

Why hadn't Andy spoken to her about it during the last week? They'd talked and talked in bed, but about the present, not the past.

About love—not bitterness…

She walked home slowly, uncertain where her husband, or their guests, might be, wanting only to be alone to think, although by now her mind was running around in circles like a demented mouse in an experimental maze.

Every thought led to a dead end.

And how could she possibly work out just what was bothering Andy about the whole baby business if she didn't know what he was thinking?

Didn't know how he had felt, for that matter…

She had a shower, which cooled her off for about ten seconds, then wandered into the kitchen to make dinner for their guests.

She had a leg of lamb in the fridge but the thought of turning on the oven in the already oven-like temperature made her shake her head.

Maybe they should have a takeaway?

She knew her thoughts about what to feed people were irrelevant but thinking about Andy was tying knots in her head so it was infinitely preferable to thinking about him.

Feeling the pain thinking about him caused.

With a huge sigh, she opened the fridge, where she found the stack of T-bone steaks the butcher had pressed on her yesterday. She decided to make a salad, brimful of lettuce and spinach and tomatoes, some avocado and a tin of chickpeas for extra protein.

And later maybe she and Andy could talk…

*She* could go to *his* room this time.

Excitement that had risen at the thought hit a wall.

What if he rejected her?

Sent her away?

She was letting her imagination run away with her, coming up with all manner of stupid scenarios.

She heard the sound of cars pulling up outside.

She splashed water on her face, aware her last imagined scenario had brought tears to her eyes, and went out to greet their guests.

Apparently, Chelsea had ducked home earlier and put clean sheets on the beds in the rooms on either side of hers, and it was there she led Jill and Harry, with Ellie trailing along behind.

'You'll probably need a shower after your travelling and the heat out here,' she said.

'There are bathrooms off your bedrooms, so feel free. And if you'd like a rest before dinner, that's fine, or you could sit on the veranda outside your room. It will be cooler there and you'll get to see a spectacular sunset.'

'That's true, Mum,' Chelsea said. 'It was like I'd never seen a sunset before until I came here.'

Ellie left them with Chelsea to settle in, covered the big salad with cling film, and set it in the fridge.

She was cleaning up the mess she'd made in the kitchen when she heard a siren, and her heart stood still.

It came from the mine outside town. Her first thought was that it was a practice drill—she'd heard it a few times before—but Ellie really knew it was too late in the afternoon to be a practice drill.

She hurried around the veranda.

'Chels, will you look after your family? Get them drinks and anything else they need. I've got to pop out for a bit. There's a salad in the fridge, and steaks for the barbecue. Can you manage dinner if I'm late?'

She hoped they wouldn't ask about the noise that was still wailing over the small town.

She escaped before they could.

Mine safety was a priority these days, the

miners might be trapped, but surely they'd be all right?

Ellie went to the hospital first, which was the rallying point for all medical staff, but one of the ambos saw her and offered her a lift to the mine.

'They say it's bad. Andy's there already and they might need you as well, Doc.'

Ellie climbed into the vehicle, telling herself there were safe places along all the tunnels in the old coal mine—places protected from rock falls, with supplies of water, biscuits, torches and even phone lines to the surface.

Any miners in a tunnel or a shaft could seek shelter there. They would all be safe.

As long as they hadn't been directly under the fall…

The first person she saw was Andy, talking to the shift engineer near the head of the main shaft.

'You don't need to be here.' he said, and she grinned at him.

'Oh, no? And you do?'

'We don't know who we'll need,' the engineer said. 'But it was good of both of you to come. The ambos are busy talking to the relatives of the men who are on shift.'

'Logan Grant's father?' Ellie asked, thinking of the little boy they'd got to know after his father had brought him around to apologise to her, and had since become a nearly constant presence around the house, digging weeds from her garden and teasing Chelsea to distraction but really loved by all of them.

The thought that he might lose his father, as well as his mother, was unbearable…

'We'll go over to the main office,' the engineer said. 'Word will come through to there first.'

But even as they left a cheer went up, and Ellie looked back to see the elevator rising up the shaft, a group of blackened men packed inside it.

Cries and questions rang out, but the on-duty manager herded them all into the washrooms, determined to keep to routine, even at a difficult time.

'Are they all up?' Ellie asked the engineer, who had also stopped to watch the spectacle.

He shook his head.

'We always knew this lot was safe. The fall was further down number five. There were another dozen men working down there.'

Ellie closed her eyes, an unconscious prayer for their safety forming in her mind.

'Have you heard from them?' Andy asked, and the engineer shook his head.

'But that doesn't mean much as the fall could

have cut the phone lines and, of course, mobiles won't work that far down.'

He paused then added, 'But remember we have one of the best mine rescue teams in the world and they are already down there, using all manner of equipment to work out the depth of the fall, and setting up listening devices to pick up any voices.'

'How do you know they're the best in the world?' Andy asked, and Ellie had to smile. It was such an Andy kind of question, wanting proof of things people told him.

'Interstate comps, then world competitions, believe it or not,' the engineer said. 'Our team won the international title three years in a row.'

'Of course,' he added, 'underground mining is fast being phased out. It's nearly all open cut now, and not much of that going on as the power companies have begun experimenting with cheaper, renewable energy options.'

He led them into the office and showed them, on a map on the wall, just where the miners were trapped.

'There's an air shaft just here,' he said, pointing to a windmill-shaped symbol, 'so they should be getting air.'

*If* they'd made it to the safety bay, Ellie thought, but didn't say, aware everyone was probably thinking the same thing.

Another man approached them, carrying overalls and safety helmets. He helped them into the heavy, fire-retardant overalls, and showed them how to switch on the lamps on their helmets.

Swamped by the overalls, Ellie was bent over, rolling up the legs, when Andy touched her shoulder.

'Let me,' he said, and squatted down, doing a far neater job than she'd been doing.

'Now your arms. Hold them out.'

He rolled up the sleeves, then patted the pocket where she knew from drills the heavy gloves were kept.

'Remember they're there if you need them,' he said sternly, and even though she didn't think she'd be digging through coal and actually require them, she smiled as she thanked him. It was nice having Andy fussing over her…

Once dressed for action, she and Andy stood, a little apart from the professionals, who all appeared to know exactly what they were doing.

So it was a rise in the level of the excitement of the men in the room—the managerial *and* engineering staff—that told them there must be some news.

After some discussion, one of the engineers crossed to speak to them.

'We've found five at the near end of the fall,'

he said quietly. 'The men are still digging them out but—'

'We're happy to go down and treat them before they're moved. They'll need to be stabilised at the very least,' Ellie told him, before Andy had time to suggest he go alone.

'If you're sure,' the man said, and although Andy shook his head at her, Ellie nodded.

'This way!'

He led them briskly out of the office towards the elevator that would take them down the shaft. Two of the ambulance crew were already there, carrying their bulging backpacks of emergency equipment and drugs.

The elevator was well lit but even so, what light escaped the cage-like structure was absorbed by the inky blackness outside so it was only when they reached the bottom and walked out into a well-lit, cavernous area that Ellie was able to get an idea of the scale of the operation.

'You should have stayed up top,' Andy murmured to his stubborn wife, as a coal-blackened miner gave orders to the rescuers. 'There's the rescue team, probably all paramedic trained, *and* the ambos—'

'*You* came,' she pointed out, stabbing him in the chest with a forefinger, 'yet you expect me not to!'

He *had* to smile.

'Not *expect* exactly, I just would have preferred, wished, in fact. I hate to think you might be in danger, Ellie, you must know that, for all that's been going on between us.'

He rested his hand lightly on her arm, wanting suddenly to be holding her; for all his anger to be gone, and the two of them be one again.

But he could hardly give her a cuddle in front of this audience, and after the way he'd reacted to her happy announcement, she'd probably slap him.

But his heart ached for her, whilst his body was tense with concern.

She really shouldn't be here…

Not that he'd win that argument if he raised it. As if his Ellie would have held back when medical assistance might be needed.

*His* Ellie?

Well, she was and as soon as this business was over he was going to sort it out.

'They're over here,' a voice was saying. 'We've propped the area so it's safe to work there.'

The man who'd spoken led them further into the mine, coming eventually to an area lit now by bright LED floodlights. Five coal-darkened figures lay on the ground. A paramedic was kneeling by one, a miner by another, while one of the ambos took another.

'One each,' Andy said, and reached out to grab Ellie's hand and give it a good squeeze.

He watched as Ellie took the closest man, and moved on to a big fellow whose legs appeared to be still trapped by the fallen rocks. Setting down his medical bag, he pulled on blue nitrile gloves.

'I'm Andy,' he said. 'Can you hear me? What's your name?'

The man nodded to the first question and offered up his name as Jason.

Andy slipped his fingers around Jason's wrist to feel his pulse.

Fast but not too fast.

'I'm going to check you over but, first, are you feeling pain anywhere?'

'Everywhere, mate,' the man said. 'Except my legs. Can't feel them at all. Shoulder's bad, and m'head. Stupid hard hat came off.'

Aware that being able to speak in sentences meant the man's airways must be working, Andy started a search for blood. He probed all around his patient's head, checking his hands for any sign that there was bleeding.

Nothing.

No sign of swelling, and no grating noises suggesting a skull fracture.

He moved on to the shoulder, stripping open the man's overalls to see his skin. Dark with coal but not with blood. But when he lifted Jason's right arm to test his shoulder, a yowl of pain stopped him short.'

'Bloody roof came down on me there,' Jason told him. 'That's when m'hard hat came off.'

Suspecting a dislocation, Andy rested his patient's arm across his chest, and pulled out what was now known as the magic green whistle, an inhaler of methoxyflurane, which would help the pain now and especially when they moved him onto a stretcher to get him out of the cramped tunnel, already filled with too many people.

'Just suck on it. A few sucks will help the pain now and you can use it again when they move you,' he said, aware the device gave metered doses and Jason couldn't hit himself with it all at once.

He continued his examination by feeling down the man's back and onto his thighs.

Here, two miners were carefully lifting lumps of rock from Jason's legs, working with great care in case one wrong move brought more rocks down.

'We should have him out in a few minutes,' they said, 'but we reckon his legs'll be okay because these rocks slid from the main fall, not directly from the roof, so he'll have cuts and bruises, but with luck nothing broken.'

And no major vessel bleeding freely, Andy hoped.

He pulled a pad from his bag and wrote: 'Conscious, query dislocated shoulder, no obvious bleeding.'

He stopped there, because the rescue team was about to remove the last rocks from Jason's feet.

'Can you move your feet?' he asked Jason, who carefully lifted first one foot and then the other.'

'You bloody beauty,' he said to his rescuers, raising his good hand for a high five with each of them.

'Stretcher needed,' Andy called, and two ambos came hurrying over.

Andy added 'Given self-administered methoxflurane' to his note, wished Jason well, and moved over to check the next patient.

'See to the chap who's with your wife,' the paramedic told him. 'This bloke's under control.'

Andy knelt beside Ellie, who had the man's chest bare and was counting down his ribs, a large-gauge needle in her hand.

'Haemothorax,' she said briefly, stabbing the

needle into a cleaned patch on the man's chest, then watching as blood and air escaped.

Andy found a catheter and handed it to her so she could slip it in over the needle as she withdrew it. He watched as she taped the little tube securely in place, attached a water seal to stop air entering the tube, and covered it with a light dressing.

'Other injuries?' he asked, as she squatted back on her heels.

'He might have a dislocated knee. He fell very awkwardly. I gave him light sedation before I stuck a needle in his chest so he's not feeling pain at the moment.'

'Are you happy for him to go?' Andy asked, and Ellie nodded, then, as he called for a stretcher, she caught his arm.

'It's no good sending people to the hospital if you're not there,' she said. 'You go back, and at least triage them so you know who will need to be sent to the hospital at Croxton, and who might need to be airlifted out for specialist treatment.'

'But you'd be useful at the hospital, too,' Andy argued.

'Not as useful as I am here,' she said, in a voice he knew would withstand any argument.

# CHAPTER NINE

IT WAS CLOSE to midnight before the five safe men had been sent off to hospital, and Ellie wondered what she should do. Those badly injured would be sent out to bigger hospitals, so Andy wouldn't need her help.

Should she go home and feed the visitors, although she guessed Chelsea would probably have done that already. Who'd wait until midnight for their dinner?

And if they'd heard about the mine accident they were likely to be in the crowd she'd heard were clustered around the fence outside the mine.

People with more knowledge than she had would be keeping them updated, so…

'Can you stick around?' a burly miner asked her.

'Of course,' she said. 'What can I do?'

She saw white teeth flash as he smiled at her.

'Right now, not a lot. There's a camp bed

through here...' He led the way back towards the lift, to an open, high-ceilinged area with tunnels branching off it.

'This is the nerve centre of the rescue operation now,' he said. 'Grab some sleep while you can. The rescue men are clearing from the top, but they have to drill supports into the roof as they go so it doesn't collapse again. This means it could be some time until we clear the blockage. But the engineers are drilling a smaller hole through the lower part so they can thread a wire through and regain contact with the men on the other side.'

Ellie was pleased to hear he was positive there *were* men safe on the other side.

'Once we've got contact with them,' her informant explained, 'we can find out about injuries. You'd be very useful telling them how to treat their injured, or even just talking to them. A woman's voice, you know...'

His voice trailed away lamely, worrying Ellie because he no longer sounded quite as positive.

'How long have you been down here?' she asked him.

'Eleven hours. I was just coming off shift when it all came down.'

'Then my first advice for treatment is that you go up top, get some food and a hot drink and if you absolutely refuse to go home, at least lie down for a while to rest your body for an hour or two. We don't need any more casualties.'

To her surprise, the man headed off towards the lift. He must have been exhausted.

Although he did turn back halfway.

'And you have a rest, too, lassie. It's going to be a very long night.'

Ellie took his advice, and was surprised to find she had fallen asleep on the camp bed and, in fact, she'd slept quite deeply.

Had it been the rattle of cups and the clunk of huge teapots, the sound of things being unwrapped, and the smell of muffins that had woken her?

Whatever the case, she'd woken in time for breakfast.

Ellie took a short break in the bathroom near the lifts, washing her face and running her fingers through her tangled hair.

'We're nearly through with the communication cable,' one of the engineers said to her, 'and we'll soon find out how the guys are.'

It still seemed to take for ever for the small hole to be drilled through the fall, but eventually the engineers were able to speak to the survivors on the other side.

'Two injured,' the man on Ellie's end of that fragile wire said. 'One badly.'

'I'm putting the doctor on the line,' she heard him say, then took the old black receiver and held it to her ear, introducing herself as Ellie in response to Dave at the other end.

'It's Eddie,' he said. 'He's lost his hard hat and there's blood all over his face, and he's mumbling at us.'

'It may be less serious than it seems,' she told Dave. 'Head wounds bleed a lot, even from small injuries.'

'Okay!'

'Is he breathing?'

'Yes, and he's got a pulse. We checked that first.'

'Are you in a safety area and if so, what first-aid things have you got?'

'There's a big red box with lots of wrapping type stuff,' Dave told her.

'Something you can use to clean him up? There'll be sterile water in little clear plastic packs. Just rip the tops off them, and wet the cloth and try to clear all the blood from around the wound. Go gently so you don't worsen the injury.'

There was silence for a while, although she could vaguely hear conversation in the background, presumably Dave giving orders to the other men.

'Doing that,' he said. 'It seems the wound is on his head at the hairline above his right eye.'

'Have someone keep pressure on it with a pad of cotton while you feel gently around it. See if there's a lump from the bump.'

'Not much of one.'

'Okay!' Ellie was thinking fast.

'Now run your fingers all over his head, gently but firmly. You're feeling for any movement in his skull or swelling anywhere else.'

Silence as the man felt his mate's head, but Ellie had thought of something that should help.

She turned to one of the men clustered near her.

'Do you have one of the big red first-aid boxes somewhere here?' she asked, and watched as someone ducked away, returning with the box and setting it at her feet.

She opened it up and was surprised at the amount of first-aid equipment in it, the contents listed by number on a sheet of paper inside the lid.

She was checking the contents when a voice said, 'He seems all right.'

'Okay! Now I have a box with me. Do you see the green gauze pads labelled twelve and a rolled bandage labelled twenty-four?'

'Got 'em both,' her new friend at the other end of the line said cheerfully.

'Then use the gauze to cover the wound and keep it there by wrapping the bandage around his head. The bandage is self-adhesive so when you've done a few firm turns just cut it off and it will stick to itself and stay there.'

She waited while Dave gave instructions for the bandage, then said, 'I need you to take his pulse again. Can you time it? Does one of you have a watch with a second hand.'

They must all be able to hear her voice for several voices offered the use of theirs.

'Then count the beats. You need only do it for half a minute then double it to get beats per minute.'

'It's very hard to feel, it's kind of weak.'

'Try the carotid artery just below the angle of his jaw. If you feel around there, you should get it.'

'Tom's got it! He's the fit one of us, he goes to the gym and takes his own pulse all the time to make sure he's alive. He says it's ninety.'

'Not too bad,' Ellie said, trying desperately to picture the situation at the other end of the line.

'Has he any other injuries that you can see or feel?'

'No, we checked that first of all. Just all the blood on his head.'

'Okay, now, is he conscious? Can you ask him his name?'

'He just mumbles. He must hear our questions because we asked him earlier where he hurt and those kinds of things, and made him move his feet and hands, but anything he says isn't making sense.'

Ellie thought she heard a mumbled protest at this stage, but it seemed he'd been lucky, and escaped with nothing more than concussion.

'I want you to keep talking to him, keep him responding even if it's only mumbles. It's probably just concussion from the knock on the head, but don't move him anyway.'

She was about to pass the phone back to the man who'd given it to her when she remembered someone had said there were two injured behind the fall.

'Who's the other injury?' she asked.

'Oh, that's Pete, but he's nearly always injured.'

The men's laughter came clearly through the phone.

'In what way?' Ellie asked.

'Ankle this time! His boot got stuck in the fall and we had to dig him out. We've taken off the boot and bound his ankle up. There's instructions in the first-aid box about bandages and things, and we just did what it said and told him to sit down and shut up his whining while we looked after Eddie.'

'There are painkillers in the box inside a blue plastic box. The ones labelled eight are paracetamol. You could give him two of them, and another two after four hours, but no more than eight in twenty-four hours.

'Yep, I can see them, but he says they're no better than spit and he needs something stronger.'

'You could give him a couple of those to begin with,' Ellie said firmly. 'And if you really believe he needs more pain relief, the tablets labelled ten are codeine and paracetamol, but you're still looking at no more than eight in twenty-four hours, and that's counting the first two.'

'He's grumbling that there should be something stronger. He's saying there should be morphine.'

'There probably is,' Ellie told him, having already found some in her red box. 'But we don't know how he'd react to it, so it's best administered by a doctor.'

'I reckon you're right. We'll keep an eye on him and if he starts to look bad, we'll talk to you about it.'

'Sounds good,' she said, then hesitated for a moment.

'Is Logan Grant's dad with you?' she asked.

'That's me,' a new voice said. 'You're Dr Ellie, aren't you?'

'I am, and I'm very pleased to hear your voice. I'll get on to your babysitter. If she can't manage the kids, they can come to my place. I've got some adults staying there who should be able to handle them.'

'Handle young Logan, you've got to be kidding!' someone said, and Ellie smiled.

'One of my visitors is a six-foot-tall rugby player. Logan might just have met his match.'

'Thank you!' Logan's father said. 'I've been worried to death about them. Our young babysitter is good, but overnight is hard, and Logan runs rings around her even in the daytime. As you know.'

'Well, rest assured they'll be well looked after.'

She checked on the welfare of the rest of the men, then phoned Andy.

'Will you tell Jill to expect the kids? Chris is here somewhere. I'll get him or Zeke to help them pack a few things and take them over to our place. Just warn Harry that Logan needs careful watching.'

'They'll all be okay,' Andy told her. 'I've got some old video games Logan might like to play, and Jill's already getting grandmotherly about Chelsea's baby so they'll be good practice for her.'

There was silence for a moment, before Andy continued, 'Are you all right? Are you still in the safe assembly area?'

Ellie had just assured him she was when a noise like thunder rolled along the tunnels, and she quickly hung up lest Andy hear it and start to worry.

She waited, wondering what had happened, but no one around her seemed particularly alarmed, until someone snapped, 'Hey, watch what you're doing!'

The voice came from one of the men stabilising the tunnel ceiling and it wasn't so much the words as an ominous creaking that had everyone move forward.

'Keep back!'

The sharp command had Ellie backing as quickly as she could, though she could still hear the man in charge, only this time he was speaking on the phone.

'You guys back there—you're all in a safety pod, aren't you? Right in it?'

Affirmative noises came through, and Ellie wondered just what was happening to make everything much more urgent.

The creaking noise had stopped, but somehow the silence seemed much louder.

'What's happening?' she murmured to the man closest to her.

'Something's moving and we don't know whether it's this end or the other.'

'Or in another tunnel altogether,' someone offered.

As all but the trapped men were out of the mine, Ellie realised the danger must be to those trapped, hence the questions about where they were.

The rescue team working on securing the top of the tunnel had retreated towards the group at the lifts, then another roaring noise filled the air with dust, which finally settled to reveal a further fall.

The men in charge began discussing what this meant, and as far as Ellie could make out, the prediction was that they would have to work more slowly and it could be another two days before they freed the men.

And their fragile telephone link to the men was no longer working.

'We should get you back up to the top,' someone said, realising Ellie was still in their midst. 'Although…'

He paused.

'Although?' Ellie prompted.

'I was thinking of the air shaft.'

'You can't ask a woman to go down that,' one said.

'And a small worker could do it just as easily,' another added.

'But there are injured men in there,' Ellie reminded them, 'and we've only got reports that they're okay. I'm happy to go in that way. After all, it's only two days until they're free, you say. I'll be home for Christmas!'

The group of men moved a little away from her as a furious, whispered argument took place but in her heart she knew she should be the one to go.

Even Andy called her a skinny little runt at times. This was a time when size *did* matter.

'I'll go,' she told them. 'Just tell me what I need to do.'

The whole group was now looking at her.

She smiled at them.

'I'm happy to do it.'

'You'll need a canister of air and a mask over your face. The air vent will be lined with coal dust that'll be everywhere once you disturb it,' one of the engineers told her. 'I'll send a team up to clear the machinery at the top of it. And we'll have you double roped, with one rope attached to a safety harness and another you can stand on as you go down.'

He seemed excited, but worry was creeping

into his voice again as he discussed the practical side of things.

'Are you *quite* sure?'

'I am,' she assured them all. 'But I'll need a few things lowered down as well. My medical bag, and perhaps a container of water, and some chocolate as treats for the men. I could go first and you could lower other stuff down to me.'

And although he'd been the one to send the order about removing the machinery from the top of the shaft, the engineer still seemed doubtful.

'What if it's blocked?' he said.

'Then you can pull me up,' she told him, 'but you know it isn't blocked. The men have told us the air is fresh.'

'You're a champ,' someone said, while another man patted her shoulder.

Then everyone was moving, some taking Ellie back to the surface in the lift, and as they did so were discussing the mechanics of what lay ahead.

It was probably best if she didn't listen to that part.

Again, she considered phoning Andy, but she knew he'd forbid it, and then be furious with her for doing it anyway.

Besides, he'd worry…

* * *

Andy heard the news from Chris when he delivered Logan and his sisters to the house.

'She's going down an air shaft? Whoever thought of such a crazy idea? Nobody knows if they'll get those men out of there. She could be trapped. There could be another fall!'

Chris's reassurances that all would be well and that the mine engineers had it all under control fell on deaf ears as panic spread through Andy's body.

His imagination was only too willing to supply him with plenty of 'worst' scenarios: Ellie trapped in the air shaft; another rockfall; the trapped men… He couldn't—or wouldn't—think of any scenarios including them…

His heart was stuttering in his chest, and for all he knew there were things he should be doing, like calling Maureen to cancel the morning's patients, but his mind couldn't move past the image of his wife trapped a mile or so beneath the ground.

And suddenly all they'd been through seemed so trivial he could have cried. The time they'd wasted, the pain they'd caused each other. What if something happened and he couldn't hold her again, tell her he loved her, explain his panic about having another baby?

Moving like an automaton, Andy did what had to be done: he saw to the guests; phoned Maureen; and finally went back to work. Not that he could stay there, not when his wife was—

No, he wasn't going to start that again, but at least if he waited at the mine, he'd hear all the latest news, maybe even get a message to her. Would they send a message saying 'I love you'?

And would that be enough when there was so much more he needed to say?

He told Andrea to contact him if he was needed, and headed back out to the mine.

Offering to be lowered down a long, dark ventilation shaft was one thing. Doing it, Ellie soon realised, was entirely different. For a start, it wasn't a darkness she'd ever experienced before. It was as if the blackness was physical so it seemed to press against her.

And the shaft seemed to grow narrower as she went down, although she knew this was her imagination.

Then light appeared and before she knew it, eager hands were helping her stand on firm earth again, undoing her harness and generally welcoming her presence.

She stepped away from them and stripped off the filthy overalls she'd worn down the shaft, which were now black with coal dust.

'We'd better stand clear, there's more coming,' she said, and smiled when the men looked puzzled.

'Extra water because I thought Pete's ankle might need an open cast.'

She waited until the bundle arrived before mentioning chocolate, which had the desired effect of lifting the men's spirits, especially as it came in the form of little chocolate Santas.

Her rescuers clustered around her and the only one she recognised, Logan's dad, gave her a hug.

'Hey, I'm the patient here,' someone complained, and Ellie guessed it was Pete, lying on the floor with his ankle bandaged.

'I'll just check Eddie then come back to you,' Ellie promised.

Eddie was still and quiet, but as far as Ellie could tell the injury hadn't been severe, and the pupils in both eyes reacted equally to light.

'Just sit by him in case there's any change,' Ellie told the man nearest to her. 'You can talk to him if you like, or not. He'll have a crashing headache and might not feel like responding. But stay near him, check his pulse every ten minutes or so, and let me know if anything changes.'

She looked at the few men clustered around her.

'You can do that? Take turns?' she asked,

and was assured they'd stay close to him, one of them settling beside Eddie to begin telling him a long story about when they were kids, asking Eddie questions to which he sometimes mumbled an answer—or what might have been an answer.

Ellie went to kneel beside Pete, handing him a green whistle to suck while she unwrapped the bandage.

She suspected he could have broken the ends of his tibia and fibula when the rocks had landed on him, which meant he had reason to complain. She'd checked the big red box before she'd come down the air shaft, and knew there was treated cloth in it. She could fashion it into an open cast for his ankle and lower leg, and hold it in place with the bandages.

It would allow for swelling and its rigidity would prevent further displacement of the bones.

It took all her concentration to get it right, but around her she could hear the jokes and quips of the men and was pleased at how high their spirits seemed to be, although, to a certain extent what was to her a grim, dark, rather frightening tunnel was a second home to them.

With both patients checked, Ellie turned her attention to the other men. Kane Grant in particular was showing evidence of stress.

'My family will take good care of your children,' she told him, but it didn't ease his concern. His main lament was that he should have got a different job so he could be at home more often with his children.

'But any job will take you away from them for part of the day,' Ellie reminded him, 'and mining's been your life.'

'But Logan's going to be in trouble wherever he goes,' Kane lamented. 'I should have done better with him.'

Ellie knew she had to listen but other men had worries as well.

'When did you last sleep?' she asked Kane, who shook his head.

'I've no idea! I've been sleeping badly even at home and haven't slept down here since the cave-in.'

Ellie opened her own bag and found an anti-anxiety drug to give him. Even if it didn't make him sleep it would calm his nerves.

Kane accepted the tablet and the water Ellie offered him, then took her advice and went over to one of the hammocks the men had rigged up out of their overalls, climbed in, swung back and forth a bit, then fell deeply asleep, unaware of the men setting up a game of poker practically underneath him.

And life underground settled into a strange

kind of normality, with everyone taking turns to sleep in the two rigged hammocks, Ellie listening to stories of other hair-raising events in the miners' lives, playing cards, telling jokes. Kane Grant, his anxiety abated, revealed a wonderful supply of limericks and short poems, some of which, Ellie was sure, he cleaned up for her benefit.

The breakthrough came earlier than they'd expected, and once one man came through others followed, helping the trapped man over the still-existing mound of rubble, and out to waiting health professionals on the other side.

Ellie waited until they'd all been taken up, then one of the engineers insisted she go topside herself.

As she rode up for what seemed like for ever, the tiredness she'd managed to keep at bay crept over her, and though she obediently trudged through the shower rooms and out through the clean room, she wondered how she'd have the strength to get home.

Until familiar arms folded about her, and Andy drew her close, his body shaking with emotion as he held her, whispering her name like a prayer.

'Oh, Andy, thank you for coming,' she said, as she disentangled herself.

'You don't have to thank me for anything,' he

said gruffly. 'I've been going out of my mind with worry about you, about something happening to you before I could talk to you and make things right between us. I came because I needed to see you, and hold you, and say I'm sorry I've been such an idiot and caused you so much pain.'

He paused before adding, 'Not that you haven't caused me the torment of the damned these last few days. I *do* understand you felt you had to go, but the agony of not knowing what was happening down there... Perhaps I deserved it for being an ass.'

He was leading her towards the outer fence where he'd obviously parked the car, and although his conversation was confusing she was so grateful for his supporting arms, she didn't try to make sense of it.

It was enormously comforting and that was enough.

'It was the baby—our baby!' he said, as he settled her into the car and then got into the driver's side himself and continued without losing a beat.

'I was devastated. I'd never felt pain like it, but I knew I had to be strong for you, so I just kept going. I know now—I've been talking to people on help-lines—that I should have dealt with it instead of just shoving it aside until it became such a big thing in my subconscious mind. The very thought of another baby—another possible loss—brought back all that stuff so strongly…'

'You couldn't bear the thought of it happening again?' Ellie said softly.

'Exactly! I thought I couldn't handle it or look after you when I knew it would paralyse me.'

She reached out a hand and held it against the strong column of his neck.

'And it took me being down in a big hole with a lot of very dirty miners for you to figure it out?'

He turned with a slightly shamefaced grin.

'I did worry about you being down there, but I'd been on to the helplines before that. I contacted them when I had that stupid reaction to something you'd said with so much love and happiness, about a miracle chance of a pregnancy. I went to pieces and knew I needed help, so I went looking for it.'

'And got it?'

He smiled and nodded.

'I'll keep having counselling sessions with the person they've found for me—there's a lot of ugly stuff to get through, but never doubt my love for you, my Ellie.'

He'd drawn over to the side of the road and halted the car, sliding the gear stick into Park so he could take her in his arms again and kiss her, gently at first, then with increasing passion.

'I should have known how you were feeling,' she said quietly, but he shook his head against her neck.

'*I* should have shared,' he said. 'Stupid macho posturing, that's all it was, and it caused us both so much pain and wasted so many months of our lives together.'

Ellie held him tightly, feeling the tension drain from his body as he talked.

But how could she *not* have known?

Whatever, it must never happen again, and now he'd spoken of the depths of his grief and despair when they'd lost the baby, she could understand him never wanting to go through something like that again.

Could she understand and accept?

In her head, she shrugged.

Of course she'd accept. She loved Andy more than life itself and to know she'd caused him pain…

'We'd better get home,' he said, slowly disentangling himself from her arms and the bits of car that had been sticking into him. 'You've no idea what a circus we've got there, but Jill and Harry have been wonderful. They not only fed me, but they've been sending boxes of sandwiches up to the mine for people waiting for news. Is this it now—everyone out?'

Ellie smiled at him. Her body was still tight with emotions she'd have to sort out one day, but ordinary chat was just what she needed right now.

'Everyone, and only two a bit the worse for wear. Logan's dad, Kane Grant, is emotionally fragile. I've asked him to bring the kids and come to us for Christmas dinner.'

Andy nodded, and Ellie continued, 'And I thought I'd ask Jill and Harry to stay on for Christmas, rather than driving back to Sydney in all the Christmas holiday traffic. It'd be a two-day drive for them, so why not stay and we can all celebrate together?'

Andy laughed.

'I daren't even begin to count how many that will give us. It will be Jill and Harry and Chelsea. But after Christmas Jill wants Chelsea home, and will home-school her if Chels decides she can't face school.'

'That's not so bad, just add the four Grants and us—that's nine, which is a great number for a real family kind of Christmas.'

# CHAPTER TEN

EXPECTING CHAOS, ELLIE was pleasantly surprised to arrive home to a quiet house that welcomed her not only because it was home but because someone—Jill most probably—had arranged fresh flowers from the garden in every room in the house.

And everyone was out.

A note on the kitchen table explained that.

*Thought you might like the house to yourself, so we've all gone off to the Thai and then to a movie. Join us if you like, but I'm thinking you'll be tired.*

*I'm sorry my family seems to have taken over your life, but we can pack up and go to a motel if you would prefer.*

*Love, Chelsea*

Bless the girl! Ellie thought, walking around the spotless house, smelling the faint fragrance of the flowers, and wondering why it was taking Andy so long to put the car away.

She heard him coming before she saw him, huffing and puffing up the back steps.

'What is Christmas without a tree?' he gasped, plonking a decent-sized cypress pine down on the floor of the veranda.

'Oh, Andy, it's beautiful. I had no idea we could get a live tree out here.'

'I'll have you know that they grow out here, my girl,' he said. 'One of the porters at the hospital has a small stand of them on his property and he brought it in for me—well, for us!'

'Let's decorate it now!' Ellie said, and Andy groaned.

'They must have been feeding you down in that hole in the ground, but I'm starving and unless I was mistaken, Jill was going to leave a casserole in the fridge. We need only bung it in the microwave and perhaps have a glass of something while we wait for it to heat.'

'But—' she began, but Andy cut her off.

'But nothing. Come and sit on the veranda with me while it heats. I've a very nice bottle of bubbly in the cooler out there.'

They ate on the veranda, but although the food was delicious, Ellie couldn't manage much, the stress of her underground days catching up with her.

Andy cleaned up after their dinner, while Ellie showered again, this time in her own bathroom, with her own soap and shampoo, then she slipped into bed, a little uncertain.

Would Andy join her there?

Were the problems of the past really behind them?

She still felt bad that she hadn't known how much he'd struggled with their baby's death, and wondered if he'd blamed her for not knowing.

But he did join her in bed, and as his hands slid over her body, each touch a silent word of love, she discovered she wasn't as tired as she'd thought she was. They made love slowly, teasing each other with kisses, until they joined in a cataclysmic release that wiped away all the pain, and doubts, and remembered loneliness, reaffirming the love they'd always known existed but had somehow lost its way in sorrow, and taken time to find again.

Bright and early next morning, Ellie made her way to the kitchen to find all their guests in occupation, and a vast array of freshly baked rolls, tubs of yoghurt, and bowls of fresh fruit set out on the table.

'You must think we're terrible,' Jill said. 'Taking over your home while you've been helping the miners. Please take whatever you like for breakfast.'

Ellie helped herself to yoghurt and cut mango, talking as she grabbed a couple of rolls to sustain her through the morning.

'I'm just glad you're here,' she said. 'You've kept Andy's mind off what was happening in the mine, done a huge amount of shopping so we can all eat, and put flowers everywhere. Thank you so much. The roses are always so lovely in summer but I never seem to get time to do anything with them.'

'You've such a lovely garden and the roses are so beautiful I couldn't resist.'

Ellie thanked her again, adding, 'I really should get back to work. Heaven only knows how all my patients have been managing.'

'If you're going to be busy you don't want all of us staying here,' Jill said in a no-nonsense voice.

'Of course we do. Andy told me he'd invited you for Christmas and I'm really looking forward to having a crowd. It would have been very lonely for just Andy and me when we've always had family Christmases.'

And especially when she'd have kept thinking of the baby who wasn't with them. She closed her eyes, remembering that terrible time when it had seemed as if their world had crashed to pieces around them, and how Andy hadn't been able to share his grief.

'But what we do need to do, Jill, is count heads and work out food. I've asked Kane Grant and his three kids.'

'And I thought we might ask Zeke.'

This from Chelsea, turning a little pink as she mentioned the young policeman's name.

'So add it all up,' Ellie told her. 'I make it ten so we need to see the butcher and ask if he can get us a large turkey and ham at this late stage. I'd prefer a turkey buffe—you know, the ones that are just the breasts—but we might need the whole thing to feed us.'

'We'll sort that out,' Jill assured her, as Ellie checked her watch and knew she should have been gone ten minutes earlier.

Maureen greeted her with a big hug.

'I don't know how you did it,' she said. 'My husband's a miner and I went down once, but never again. Talk about claustrophobia.'

'But it's as big as a cathedral down there where the lift ends,' Ellie protested. 'There were trucks down there.'

She didn't mention the shaft or the fact that it had given her many uneasy moments, or the cramped safety bunker they'd all crowded into.

'It's still under the ground and unnatural for

anyone but a rabbit or wombat,' Maureen said, before handing over messages and sending a list of patients through to Ellie's computer.

One of the messages was from Madeleine Courtney, thanking Ellie for the referral to the specialist, who had given her so much information she knew she'd be able to handle her lupus much better now.

Ellie was thrilled, that was one problem solved, and she didn't need to worry about Madeleine any more.

The day began…

Andy walked around his small domain, assuring himself that there really wasn't anything he could do here.

With only two days to Christmas most patients had made sure they were well enough to go home, and even most of the elderly had gone to relatives.

And if he went home he could decorate the tree and house and surprise Ellie.

*Ellie.*

How close had he come to losing her?

He didn't know the answer to that question, but just the thought that it might have happened made him feel ill.

He told the hospital manager where he'd be

and walked home, the morning sun just warming up for another very hot day.

His tree wasn't looking too perky, having been abandoned on the veranda floor all night, but once he'd managed to pack it, upright, into a bucket of wet dirt, it looked a lot better.

The box of the family's old decorations was still on the veranda, so he dragged it closer to the tree then realised that this had always been a job his sisters had done. How the hell did you decorate a Christmas tree?

*Can't be that hard*, he decided, and began to strew the contents of the box around it on the floor, seeking something like a length of tinsel or maybe fairy lights to wind around it for a start.

There was nothing.

Had his mother decided to throw away anything that looked too tattered?

He could go up town and get some lights and tinsel, but he'd really wanted to do this as a surprise for Ellie when she finished her morning's work.

There were heaps of baubles.

Should he do a colour theme—all red or all silver, or maybe red and gold, or silver and blue? All those colours were there and he had vague recollections that the tree had always looked beautiful but not always the same.

He didn't really have time to think it through, so he set to work, hanging baubles on the tree, cursing the ones that had broken tops and wouldn't hang, moving up and down the tree so there was an even spread.

Except he was fast running out of baubles and he had the back half of the tree still to do.

Maybe Ellie wouldn't notice that, because he really wanted to get some gold angels, which he'd just discovered in a smaller box, attached here and there, and he'd found the angel for the top in another box.

*With* the fairy lights.

And underneath them, another package, wrapped in faded brown paper. He opened it carefully and stared in disbelief at the contents—one red and white Santa suit, complete with cap and beard and glasses.

He had to smile, remembering his father, when he'd been younger and slimmer, clambering into it each Christmas, and doing the rounds of the hospital and the older people's annexe, giving out chocolates.

Could he bring back the idea and make a Santa call at the hospital?

*Tree first*, he reminded himself, and began to wind the lights around his tree.

But trying to wind them around the tree *and* the baubles was far harder then he'd realised.

With three sisters, tree decoration had always been their domain, and since he and Ellie had been together, because they'd usually spent Christmas at one of their families' homes, Ellie had kept only a small tree at home. Sometimes just some twisted bits of willow, sprayed gold and decorated with odds and ends they'd picked up in their travels.

So he was standing in a tangle of wire and bulbs and baubles when he heard Ellie coming up the steps.

He stepped forward, hoping to head her off, and the tree followed him, just tilting at first, then crashing to the floor.

'I was doing it as a surprise for you,' he muttered, as she stood and laughed at the chaos.

'Well, it's certainly that!' she said, trying to stifle the giggles that kept coming.

But she came towards him and knelt beside him, all tangled in wires, on the floor. She put her arms around him, lights, baubles, tree and all, and gave him a big hug.

'Just stay still so I can untangle you,' she said, when she was done with her hugs and kisses. 'It was a lovely idea and I'm sure we can fix it up, but first let's get the lights sorted.'

She sat beside him, lifting the loops of wire over his head.

'Have you tried the lights? Tightened all the little bulbs? Found any dead ones?'

He looked blankly at her.

'You do that first,' she said, 'before you put them on the tree because, especially on older strings of light, if you've got one dead or loose bulb the whole lot doesn't work.'

Andy shook his head, then smiled and kissed her.

'Isn't it nice to be us again?'

And the simple question struck deep into her heart, forcing a lump too big to swallow into her throat, so all she could do by way of agreement was kiss him back.

Hold him and kiss him, and let all her love flow into him, while she felt his flow into her.

'Well, that must have been some kiss to have brought the whole tree down.'

The voice, coming so unexpectedly, had them moving hurriedly apart, Ellie to frown in confusion at Chelsea, who'd appeared as if from nowhere.

But Andy handled it better.

'Don't be cheeky, young lady,' he said with mock severity, 'or I'll make you clean up the mess.'

Chelsea laughed and came forward to begin the job, carefully rescuing any unbroken baubles and brushing dirt off them, setting them on the table until they could get the tree upright again.

Ellie left them to it. She wanted to have a quick snack then go back to work, making up missed appointments, so she could be home in time to have dinner with her visitors for the first time.

'Where is everyone?' she asked Chelsea, who came into the kitchen for a dustpan and brush.

'Mum's on the scrounge for Christmas stuff, and Harry's decided he wouldn't mind being a policeman so is tagging around with Chris and Zeke for the day.'

She was heading out the door when she turned.

'Do you really not mind us all being here?' she said. 'I feel dreadful. If it wasn't for my own stupidity, none of this would have happened, and you wouldn't be lumped with all the family for Christmas.'

Ellie smiled at the young woman she'd grown so fond of.

'Christmas is for families,' she reminded Chelsea. 'Andy and I would probably have been quite miserable on our own, or wouldn't have bothered much with a celebration and just treated it as an extra day off.'

She paused, thinking of the decision she'd nearly made to leave Maytown before Christmas, back before Chelsea had somehow brought happiness back into the house.

'So really you're doing us a huge favour,' Ellie said, and meant it for she knew now, as well as she knew her own name, that she and Andy were as one again.

And always would be.

Chelsea grinned and headed back to the mess on the veranda, Andy demanding to know what had taken her so long.

'Girl talk,' Ellie heard Chelsea say. 'Just girl talk!'

# CHAPTER ELEVEN

BY LUNCHTIME ELLIE had caught up on all her appointments, so she sent Maureen home and went up into the house.

She needed to find Jill and discuss the food situation.

She discovered Jill at the butcher's, discussing sausage meat and giblets for the stuffing, totally unfazed by the numbers.

'I've done Christmas for two dozen,' she said. 'I'm one of six so Christmases were enormous.'

Jill took the parcel from the butcher, refused to let Ellie pay, and led the way out the door.

'It's a good thing you've got the barbecue with a lid because we can use that as an oven to cook the ham. Now, let me look at my list.'

She produced a piece of foolscap-size paper.

'That's not a list, it's an inventory!' Ellie said, and Jill smiled.

'You just go away and do something for yourself, or have a little rest. Leave this to me.'

Having a little rest sounded like a very good idea, but she knew there'd be presents for her and Andy already under the tree from the visitors, so she needed some small gifts to give them, and something for the children, so she went shopping instead…

Christmas Eve was a day of celebration for the entire town. The rescued miners were ferried down the streets on gaily decorated utilities, each in an armchair on the tray back. Even the two injured men took part, while what seemed like the entire town turned out to cheer them.

'Whose idea was it to release the red balloons?' Andy asked Ellie when he caught up with her outside the hospital.

'Chelsea's, of course. She's had all the soccer team and half the high school population filling balloons with helium she conned out of the two-dollar shop. They've handed them out to people up and down the main road with orders to release them as the men went past.'

So the hot, dry air was filled with red balloons floating lazily above the parade, some of the miners catching hold of strings and making a bunch of them.

'You should be up on one of those chairs,' Andy told her, an arm around her shoulders.'

'More like the whole rescue team,' she reminded him. 'But I think it's nice to see them celebrated, even though it's so close to Christmas. Things tend to get back to normal so quickly and in another week or so it will be forgotten.'

'Except by the engineers and managers who'll be trying to work out why it happened,' Andy said. 'Are you heading home now?

Andy watched her walk away. She was special, his Ellie, and for about the thousandth time since they'd made up he wished he had a special gift for her.

He'd bought her favourite perfume, a couple of books by authors he knew she enjoyed, and an eternity ring because now their marriage *was* going to be for ever.

But the 'something special' he felt sure was out there had eluded him.

He headed back into the hospital, not that there was much to do, except the endless paperwork that he tended to put off until the last possible moment.

Which was today, if he wanted to take a few days off over Christmas. Not that he'd be off duty, just on call from home, although he'd do morning and evening rounds as usual.

He smiled to himself as he thought of the tree they'd finally managed to decorate, its lights shining brightly on the veranda. Not to mention the tinsel that seemed to adorn every room, and the golden bells that hung in every doorway, the fairy lights strung around the veranda railing, and the little nativity scene Jill had brought with her as a gift for him and Ellie.

Christmas was going to be special, very special!

If only he could think what to get Ellie…

The sun eventually rose on the great day—a huge red orb in the eastern sky, promising a fiery heat for foolish people sticking to the traditional roast turkey and ham of their European forebears when the temperature was in the forties.

Ellie woke early, moving quietly through the sleeping household. Chelsea's family had been to the midnight church service so she was certain they'd sleep in, while she wanted to grab a cup of tea and sit outside and think of all that had happened in the tumultuous twelve months since last Christmas.

True, she and Andy had been through sadness, and the unbelievably hard consequences of losing the baby, but wasn't their marriage all the stronger for that suffering?

Hadn't they found a whole new level of happiness, a new depth of love, in the last few weeks?

She smiled, pushing aside memories of that time when she'd thought their marriage wouldn't survive, pushing aside remembered pain and anguish.

Today was Christmas Day, a day of celebration…

'Join you?'

Andy settled beside her on the top step, set down his cup of tea, and put his arm around her shoulder.

'It's been a tough year, hasn't it, my darling, but we made it.'

She turned and kissed him.

'Indeed we did.'

She shifted so she could see him—look at him.

'You all right?' she asked, and he smiled at her.

'More than all right,' he told her, and the strength in the words told her they were true. 'And while we're on our own, there's one thing I want to do.'

Intrigued, Ellie let him pull her off the step and lead her to the tree, where he produced a parcel wrapped in gold tissue paper.

He handed it to her and for some reason her fingers shook as she unwrapped it, so it took a while to reveal the contents—an angel dressed in white, with gossamer golden wings and a golden crown.

'For our tree?' she whispered, and Andy held her and kissed her lips.

'For our tree and our baby,' he said, his voice hoarse with emotion. 'Angels were all male, you know, so shall we go and put him up, right at the top where he belongs, so we can share every Christmas with him?'

Ellie wiped the tears from her face and led the way to the tree, carefully removing the old and rather battered angel and replacing it with the new one—*their* angel.

Andy hugged her.

'*Now* we're ready for Christmas,' he said. 'It will be like old times for me, family, and whatever strays Dad or Mum picked up, all together in the dining room.'

'So maybe next year we could ask them and my family if they'd like to come out and join us. After the crowd this year, just the two of us would seem odd.'

A tiny dart of pain pierced Andy's heart. Ellie's assumption that there'd be 'just the two of us' this time next year told him she'd accepted there'd be no baby.

Had it been his confessing how hard the loss had hit him that had drawn a line under the baby idea for ever, as far as Ellie was concerned?

He didn't know, but as he could hear people stirring behind them in the house, it was hardly the time to be telling Ellie he'd quite like to try again…

Breakfast was a riotous affair, Harry telling stories of university pranks, Chelsea happily enlarging on his tales and topping them with stories of the soccer team.

And once the breakfast things were cleared away, they adjourned to sit around the tree where piles of gifts were stacked. Andy played Santa, even donning a red cap, reading out the names on the greetings tags and passing over the gifts.

It soon became apparent that Jill, as well as a gift for cookery, was a seamstress and embroiderer. For Ellie, there were half a dozen linen handkerchiefs, embroidered with a flowery E and tucked into a satin bag. Andy's gift was similar, big manly handkerchiefs with a no-nonsense A embroidered on them, but also a small, smooth, wooden box, felt lined, for cuff links or tie pins or whatever manly jewellery he might have.

'Not much,' he joked as he thanked Harry

for the beautifully crafted box. 'At least now I won't lose what I do have.'

'Well, I've brought you something to start off with,' Chelsea said, producing a small box with an opal set into a tie pin.

'I've noticed at the hospital on days when you're wearing a tie, you tuck it between the buttons of your shirt so it doesn't dangle on the patients.'

Andy laughed.

'I *do* do that,' he admitted. 'I always wear a tie if there's to be a board meeting, or someone from the Health Department visiting to check we're not using too many pens and pencils.'

'More likely ear swabs and hypodermic needles,' Kane said.

And so it went, Ellie and Andy's gifts to everyone small jars of spicy nuts and pretzels that were about the only special culinary talent Ellie had.

Lunch followed, Jill, Harry and Chelsea dishing up, Logan and his sisters ferrying the overflowing plates to the table.

And once they were all settled, party hats on heads, and feeble jokes read out, they all gave thanks for the day, and the meal before them, and began to eat.

And eat…

'It's far too delicious to leave any but I really

can't manage any more,' Ellie declared, having eaten a large serving of the main course, and three-quarters of her Christmas pudding and custard.

'In fact,' she added, 'if I didn't have the clearing up to do, I'd be staggering to my bed.'

'We'll clear up,' Jill said, but Ellie raised her hand.

'*You* will do nothing,' she declared, 'except put your feet up and catch up with Chelsea. I know you want to get away early in the morning so, later in the afternoon, when it's cooler, Chelsea and Harry can help pack the car. And for now Zeke and Logan can help me and Andy in the kitchen while the girls tidy up the discarded wrapping paper around the tree.'

'She's right, you've done a marvellous job, Jill,' Andy said, 'so please go and rest. The little general here will sort out the mess.'

'Little general indeed,' Ellie said, as she and Andy finally finished in the kitchen and retired to their bedroom, collapsing onto the bed.

'You can give me orders anytime,' Andy teased, turning onto his side so he could pull her close and kiss her.

'Mmm…nice!' Ellie said. 'And did I thank you for the lovely gifts? You didn't get that perfume at the local chemist.'

'No, and while I do try to shop locally whenever possible, the internet is a wonderful thing.'

They lay, content to be together, exchanging a kiss now and then, until Andy moved a little apart, reaching out to the bedside table on his side of the bed and producing another little parcel, wrapped in Christmas paper and tied with ribbon.

'I do have one last gift,' he said, and passed it to her. 'Well, two actually, but I'll give you this one first.'

He passed it to her.

It was a small, square box that shrieked ring, and her fingers trembled as she opened it, then tears slid down her cheeks when she saw the tiny circlet of gold and diamonds—an eternity ring!

'Because we know now our marriage is for ever,' Andy said, his voice husky and his hand shaking as he put the ring on her finger.

'I love you, Ellie, always have and always will,' he said. 'And even when we'd lost our way and started hurting each other, I knew the love was still there if we could just get past the pain.'

He put his arms around her and held her close.

'I was an idiot for not talking to you, but I felt you had so much of your own emotion to deal with that adding mine to it might sink you completely!'

'And I was stupid not to realise how much you were hurting. I was wrong to wrap myself in grief and not consider you,' Ellie whispered against his neck.'

She eased away and kissed his lips.

'Never again,' she said, and as he kissed her he echoed the words, then reached for the second gift he had for her.

'Well, you're not going to top this ring, whatever it is,' Ellie told him, over the tears of shock and waving the ring delightedly in the air so sunbeams could catch the diamonds and make them wink at her.

'No,' Andy said, and sounded serious, 'but I hope you'll think it's worth just as much—perhaps more. I hope you'll understand what it's saying to you, what *I'm* saying to you!'

He handed her the second box, and once again she felt the tremors that were going through his body.

Whatever it was, it meant a lot to Andy…

It was light in weight, a smallish rectangular box of some kind, and as she tore the paper off it and saw what it was, she sat up in bed and looked at him in wonder.

'You're giving me a pregnancy test?' she said, disbelief vying with happiness.

'You know I'm probably not,' she added.

'Or you could be,' he said. 'If not now, sometime in the future.'

Ellie knelt on the bed and took his face between the palms of her hands so she could study the man she loved to distraction.

'And you'd really be okay with it? You'd be okay, even knowing we haven't had a lot of luck so far?'

He leaned across and used his hands to draw her close and kiss her lips.

'More than okay. I'd be delighted. And, yes, things can go wrong, but I can handle that now.'

He looked deep into her eyes.

'I can handle anything. With you beside me and your love giving me strength, I can take on the world.'

He grinned at her.

'But for now, don't you need a pee?'

Ellie's hands were shaking so much as she tried to open the protective box, Andy took it from her and handed her the simple test strip.

She slid off the bed, heading for the bathroom, knowing not to expect too much, not to get excited about it. There'd been too many times…

But as she sat on the loo and stared at the strip, watching the blue line spread across its width, she could only shake her head.

She should tell Andy, call him in, but her mind was blank, her tongue and lips not working.

But he came anyway, and together they stared at the strip.

'We'll need other tests. They're not always accurate—anything could happen...'

She'd gone from speechless to babbling!

How could this be? After all the tests had said it wouldn't happen? After all the years of trying had failed?

Ellie just couldn't get her head around it! The tests weren't one hundred percent accurate...

She swiped tears from her cheeks and stared at the blue line, shaking her head and hugging her body to stop herself getting too excited over it.

Until Andy knelt beside her and put his arm around her.

'And just maybe it's right and we're going to have a baby. How's that for an unbeatable Christmas present?'

He helped her up and held her in his arms, certain that this time all would be well.

'I love you, Ellie Fraser,' he said quietly, his lips moving against the hair on the top of her head.

'And I love you, Andy Fraser,' she whispered back, the air from her words warming his chest.

# EPILOGUE

WHY HAD SHE thought asking both sets of families to come for Christmas a good idea? Ellie wondered for about the fourteenth time as she settled her just-fed son James into his cot in the downstairs flat.

She smiled at James's sleeping face, touching her fingers to the spot where the little whorl of hair—just like Andy's—was beginning to show above his left eyebrow…

Even with Andy's mother running around with lists and ticking things off, Ellie still felt there was something she'd forgotten.

Vegetables—tick. Christmas pudding—tick. Bonbons and sweets and little gifts for everyone—tick…

No, it was something different—something special—and she knew she'd forgotten it.

*Baby brain.*

Maybe it would come to her. Andy should be home soon. He was up at the hospital doing his

Santa thing again and having his photo taken with children on his knee.

She'd already taken a photo of him as Santa, holding James, and knew it was something they would do each year until James was old enough to rebel against such things.

No, whatever it was—the bright idea she'd had in the middle of the night a week ago—still eluded her, and with a heavy sigh she gave up thinking about it.

After all she'd updated the watch she'd given him last year with the computerised one, and found some opal cufflinks to match the tiepin Chelsea had given him last year, and a few silly odds and ends.

More than enough.

Besides, it was Christmas Eve and the shops would be shut soon.

*All* the shops!

Racing up the steps, she found her mother-in-law, asked her to keep an eye on James, slapped a hat on her head and headed for town.

Christmas Day dawned with a promise of some relief from the heat for the sky was covered with thick cloud, and rain from a cyclone that had crossed the coast far to the west was coming their way.

Rain was the best Christmas present of all for

the surrounding farmers, and it would freshen up the town and replenish the dams, so it was a win-win all around.

'We should get up and see to our visitors,' Ellie said, as she snuggled closer to her husband.

Andy turned over and kissed her.

'From the snuffling coming from the other room, I'd say I'd better get up and look after our visitors while you feed that ever-ravenous child we produced. How does he get so hungry when all he ever does is smile and wave his arms and legs about?'

'He's growing his brains,' Ellie replied, easing herself out of the comfort of her husband's arms. 'I'll feed him then come and join you in the kitchen.'

But once there, James already handed over to a willing grandmother, she realised breakfast was already sorted, cereal, yoghurts, fruit and toast already laid out along the veranda table for everyone to help themselves.

Breakfast done, they adjourned to the living room where the beautifully decorated tree—grandmother again responsible—was stacked around with presents.

And for someone so small, James seemed to have attracted most of them, although he was sleeping blissfully on a rug on the floor while

Ellie and Andy unwrapped his treasure-trove of gifts.

'That's far too much,' Ellie protested, as more stuffed animals appeared.

'We'll find homes for all of them,' Andy whispered to her. 'In fact, some of the toys at the hospital are getting very threadbare.'

So, gifts given and admired, there was barely time for a short walk through the decorated streets, calling Christmas wishes to neighbours and friends, before returning to eat a gargantuan meal.

The day ended with a scratch supper of whatever leftovers anyone fancied, then people wandered off to their rooms or to the veranda to watch the first drops of the promised rain arrived.

Ellie fed her son for the last time—hopefully until morning although she wasn't counting on it—had a shower, then climbed into bed beside her husband.

'I've got you something else,' she said, and felt under the bed where she'd tucked a shoebox-size parcel.

She had to laugh as Andy ripped off layer after layer of wrapping, finally arriving at a small, rectangular parcel that seemed somehow familiar.

Slowly he unwrapped it then stared in disbelief at another pregnancy test.

'So much for the contraceptive effects of breastfeeding,' Ellie said to him as he continued to stare at it in disbelief.

'Do you really think?' he said. 'After all the problems we had, could we possibly have—?'

'Another?' Ellie said quietly. 'Hand it over and we'll see.'

* * * * *

*If you enjoyed this story, check out these other great reads from Meredith Webber*

A Wife for the Surgeon Sheikh
New Year Wedding for the Crown Prince
Healed by Her Army Doc
From Bachelor to Daddy

*All available now!*